Night Of Destiny

"A Titanic Survivor Story"

BY

KELLY ANN REED

Cover Art by
Craig Reed

MICK ART PRODUCTIONS LLC
PUBLISHING

www.mickcartproductions.com

Mick Art Productions, LLC
www.mickartproductions.com
ISBN: 978-0-9827000-4-4
LOC: 2012937011

PRINTED IN THE UNITED STATES OF AMERICA

This novella is dedicated to my husband, Craig.

You have been a source of encouragement

and love to me for many years.

Thank you for believing in me.

I love you.

Kel

Prologue

I had to keep pinching myself because I could not believe the blessing that was mine. I was partaking in history by being aboard the RMS Titanic on her maiden voyage across the Atlantic Ocean. How exciting it was to be young, single, and traveling on one of the most spectacular ships ever built.

My joy knew no end the day the boarding pass arrived, permitting me to leave my job at a linen factory in Ireland, and travel to Chicago, Illinois to start life anew with some relatives living there.

How wonderfully delighted and humbled I was to find that they had secured my passage to America on such a fine and grand vessel. The whole situation just seemed too good to be true and that is why I kept pinching myself.

All my life I had dreamt of distant places, of adventure, and of daring exploits. From an early age, my addiction for the written word had me devouring books that dealt with exotic travel and exploration.

"One day," I had said time and again, "I will be part of a great excursion in which the outcome of that journey will affect others for years to come."

How little I had understood the power and creativity of the spoken word but after the events and happenings that took place on the night and morning of April 14th and 15th, 1912, I have had many opportunities to ponder on the preciseness of my prophesy. My name is Shanna Kathryn. I was twenty years old and this is my story.

Chapter 1

The RMS Titanic was the esteemed pride of the White Star Line. The 'Queen of the Ocean' is how they advertised her on their billings. She had been designed and built in such a way that a magazine article had deemed her practically unsinkable. One look at her graceful lines and solid construction and it was easy to understand why she had been termed so.

I boarded her, as a third class passenger, on April 11th in Queenstown, Ireland. I was among many who were traveling to the United States with big dreams and gigantic hopes of a bright future. The United States was the land of opportunity and the home of free enterprise. It was the place where nobodies could become somebody and the somebodies could become richer. It was a country where dreams really did come true and because of this, excitement was elevated on the third class decks. You could feel a current of expectancy radiate amongst the people as spirits were soaring high and needed little stimulation. Everyone appeared jovial and seemed really to care about their fellow man. I shall never forget this feeling as long as I live. It shall always be one of the high points of my life.

Closing my eyes, even now, I can recall the smells and sounds of that very day. The salty fragrance of the ocean, the different and unique scents of all kinds of people, the distinct odor of a new ship, and the tantalizing aroma of food being prepared somewhere onboard all mingled together to make one unforgettable bouquet of smells. Laughter and shouts of joy echoed through the companionways as we boarded and I could not help but smile. I was giddy, thrilled, and thankful to be alive. I thanked God continually for this adventure of a lifetime and as we cast off from the docks, hope sprung eternal within me and I wept with the joy I felt inside.

My cabin, which I shared with three other women who were from Ireland and traveling alone, was on E deck.

Janice was a small, shy sixteen year old with a sweet smile and creamy complexion. She had curly red hair that framed her face becomingly and eyes the color of a blue sky in summer. She, like me, was traveling to meet up with a family member in the states.

The other two girls were emigrating to America by themselves. Dark haired, gray-eyed Meghan was twenty-eight and had never been married. She was tall, thin, elegant, and educated. It was her desire to teach in a school for girls. She had two interviews to look forward to upon our arrival in New York.

Twenty three year old Eliza Mae made up the last of our foursome. She was the same height as I, about five foot eight, and had dark blonde hair worn in a chin length style and tucked behind her ears. She was a pretty girl, yet I often sensed sadness in her hazel eyes. She was relocating to New York to try to escape the nightmare she relived every time she passed by the remains of the home that once brimmed with the love of her brother, his wife, and their three children. Eliza Mae had been living with them, but had been away, taking care of an ill friend the night the fire broke out that killed the entire family. So many what ifs and could haves clouded her mind that she felt it necessary to move away. She was not sure what she would be doing once in America, but anything would be better than the constant reminder of the family she had lost.

From the moment of our first meeting, all four of us got along quite well. We took most of our meals together and spent a fair amount of time wandering the decks getting to know one another. In the passing of the days a loving friendship was cultivated; nurturing a feeling of goodwill and uniting us in companionship.

Chapter 2

Each day brought us closer to our destination and before we knew it we were in the middle of the Atlantic Ocean, only a few hundred miles from the harbor of New York.

The morning of April 14th found me standing in front of the rectangular mirror that hung upon our cabin wall giving my chestnut hair a final pat. Almond shaped brown eyes twinkled in excitement as I secured a cameo broach, which my mum had given me, to the front of my coral dress. The color did wonders for my peaches and cream complexion, and I was pleased with the overall effect of my appearance.

At that very moment, I felt on top of the world. It was Sunday and Janice and I were getting ready to attend a devotional service. I enjoyed going to church and was looking forward to the ceremony at sea.

Meghan looked up from the book she was reading as we were heading out the door. "We will wait until you return and then the four of us can go to dinner together. Is that all right with you two?"

Janice and I both nodded our heads in agreement. "That sounds wonderful." I replied, and then the two of us continued out the door.

Strolling along arm and arm, we made our way to C Deck where the service was getting ready to begin in the General Room.

There was standing room only as Janice and I made our way to the back. A small elderly woman seated at the piano began to play the introduction to the hymn, "Amazing Grace".

As the first verse was sung, I looked around in amazement. There were many nationalities represented in that room and I listened as in one accord, each sang the hymn beautifully in their own language. I had never heard such a sweet sound before. Tears sprang to my eyes when I realized that our Lord most likely thought the same thing. As one body, we praised our

God. In honor and thankfulness, we exalted Him. When the song was finished, there was not a dry eye in the room. We stood for a few moments in complete silence respecting the holiness of what had just occurred. God was in that room, and it was a glorious thing for all present.

Without a word being said, everyone clasped the hand of the person next to them. Then with radiant smiles adorning our faces, we joined in together, each in our own language, to pray the "Our Father."

It was a sweet and humble ceremony; a simple song, prayer, unity among the brethren, and God showing up. This was church at its best, who could ask for anything more? One by one, we left the service filled with joy and thanksgiving.

Janice and I wrapped our shawls around our shoulders as we roamed the deck. The morning air was chilly and you could see your breath but, the fresh air smelled good. Walking to the railing, we looked out at the expanse of ocean and gray sky. The sun was trying to break its way through the clouds and every now and then, a ray would jut down to touch the ocean's surface. Janice remarked on the beauty of the occurrence.

"It's as if, God is reaching down, ta touch the ocean with a kiss." she whispered.

Smiling at her, I squeezed her hand. "It does seem like that." I said, then shivering, inquired, "Are ye ready ta go back ta the cabin and tidy up before dinner?"

She nodded and we headed back to the entrance then moved down the stairs.

A whirr from the upper decks filtered through the air as we entered the hallway, almost sounding like music. Stopping, I grasped Janice's arm. "Can ye just imagine the men and woman all dressed in their finest, last night? Why, I can even see them as they must have danced together ta some romantic waltz."

Closing my eyes, I began to hum and then, to Janice's utter amazement, I proceeded to dance around the hall with an imaginary partner.

A moment later, she giggled and then a deep masculine Irish

voice interrupted my daydream. "Excuse me sir, but would ye be mindin' if I cut in?"

Gasping, I opened my eyes and felt hot waves of embarrassment flush over my neck and cheeks. Standing next to me, but not looking at me, but in the direction of my unseen partner, was a young man of about twenty-five. He was a tall fellow with big broad shoulders and a trim waist. His skin was deeply tanned, obviously from spending a good portion of his day in the sun, and he wore his black hair parted on the side in an unfashionably long, collar length style. The white shirt and black wool trousers with suspenders that he was wearing were nothing fancy, but he looked good in the outfit, nonetheless.

"Thank ye." He said to my invisible partner and then he turned his gaze to me and flashing me a handsome grin, held up his hand in an invitation and asked, "Shall we?"

For a moment a wave of recognition passed over me as I stood there looking at him, but I quickly dismissed it, certain I had never met this man before.

Looking up into his startling blue eyes and with my heart beating wildly in my chest, I threw caution to the wind, "Certainly, kind sir. It would be a terrible loss ta let this waltz go un-danced." Then placing my hand in his, we glided around the corridor to a melody all of our own.

Janice stood there with the biggest smile on her flushed face. She was embarrassed and excited all at the same time. I was giddy as my dashing partner whirled me around, and around that corridor, before coming to stop next to Janice. Still holding me in his strong capable arms he asked, "Would ye like a go at it lass?"

Janice's bright pink face darkened and her blue eyes widened in dismay. "Heavens no!" she exclaimed locking her hands together in front of her. Aghast she stammered, "Why there isn't even any music playing."

Surprised, my handsome escort looked about the corridor seemingly confused by this remark. Looking down at me he took a step back and in all seriousness asked, "Ye heard the music didn't ye?"

Laughing, I teased, "Oh indeed I did sir, but I was making melody in me heart long before ye showed up. Music? There was definitely music."

A big smile lit his face as he nodded his head at me in a gesture of agreement and then he gently squeezed my hand, which was still resting in his.

Goose bumps broke out all over me and I tingled with excitement. This beautiful ship, handsome young man, and our daring dance would all be part of my memories forever. I smiled at him and then very reluctantly pulled my hand out of his.

"Does sir have a name?" I inquired taking a step away and smoothing my dress.

"Just call me Amos," he answered.

Studying him, I remarked, "That's a fine Godly name. In the Bible Amos brought a message of judgment on Israel. Do ye have a message for someone?"

Smiling, Amos looked me straight in the eyes and replied, "Perhaps. Would ye listen?"

Janice giggled and I blushed. Shrugging my shoulders, I said coyly, "Perhaps."

Amos's deep laughter echoed throughout the passageway causing my face to reach a deeper hue of red. I was not good at being flirtatious. I needed to put some distance between myself and this man and the sooner the better.

Moving toward Janice, I commented, "We need ta let Amos be on his way. A big strapping laddie such as himself was more than likely enroute ta the dining room before running inta us."

"As a matter of fact I was." He grinned. "Would ye lovely ladies care ta be joinin' me for dinner?"

Janice's eyes widened and she looked at me flabbergasted, shaking her head no.

Disappointed, I, too, shook my head, "I'm sorry Amos, but we promised our cabin mates that we would dine with them. In fact, we were heading there now ta freshen up, perhaps another time?"

Amos chuckled, "Another time then. Ye ladies have an enjoyable day. It was wonderful ta be making yer acquaintance."

"The same here." stammered Janice, grabbing me by the hand and pulling me in the opposite direction. Looking over my shoulder at him, I grinned and shrugged my shoulders helplessly, before waving. "Thank ye Amos for the dance. I shall never forget it."

Smiling in return, he whispered, "Nor will I, Shanna Kathryn. Nor will I."

Chapter 3

It was only after dinner, when the four of us were making our way back to the cabin, that it dawned on me that he had said my name in parting.

"How did he know me name?" I wondered aloud.

Meghan stopped at our door and looked at me. "How did who know your name?"

Dazed, I shook my head to clear my thoughts before answering. "Amos, the man Janice and I told ye about over dinner. As we were walking away he had used me name, and I don't remember telling it ta him."

Turning to Janice I questioned, "Did ye mention me name when we were with him taday?"

Her brow furrowed in thought. "Oh Shanna Kathryn, I do not believe I did, but I was so flustered by what took place that I cannot say for sure. I was a bundle of nerves the whole time we were in his presence, with him being so handsome and all. I may have said yer name. I just cannot recall right now if I did or did not."

Eliza Mae sat down on her bottom bunk and said, "Maybe he saw ye when we were out and about on one of the previous days. He could have overheard our conversation or something."

Shaking her head Janice replied, "If this man had been in the general vicinity ta over hear what we were saying, we would have definitely noticed him. He has ta be the most remarkable man I have ever seen- and tall. This man wrote the book on tall. No. If he were nearby, we would have noticed. The first time I have ever seen him was taday."

Meghan shrugged her shoulders and sat down next to Eliza Mae. "Maybe he saw you from a distance on one of the other days and felt that you were someone he would like to meet. Perhaps he found out what cabin you were lodging in and asked one of the stewards for the names of the women occupying it."

Shaking my head I concluded, "There are four girls in here. How would he have known who was who? Besides, I don't think the stewards would give out the names of their female passengers just ta anybody."

"She's right." agreed Eliza Mae. "They wouldn't have. Janice must have said it and he picked up on it. That is the only explanation."

"That is probably true." Janice agreed. "I must have used yer name and was just too flustered ta remember doing so."

It was not upsetting to me that he knew my name, quite the contrary. I felt relaxed being with him. I could not really explain it any better than to say; I believed he posed no threat. It was strange, but not. For the time being, I would just have to believe that Janice had mentioned it. Hopefully, the next time I got the opportunity to speak with him, I could ask him. Secretly, I desired another chance to see him again, and be near him. Shaking off where my thoughts were going, I grabbed a book and climbed into my top bunk to have a relaxing read.

For the remainder of the afternoon the four of us stayed in our cabin napping, talking, and sharing our hopes and dreams of what our arrival in the United States would mean.

As we opened up to one another, Eliza Mae appeared a little light-hearted as she shared with us her desire of working in a pastry shop. She had always wanted to learn how to decorate cakes for special occasions. "I love ta bake and make food look pretty. In America I believe I will get that opportunity."

"Dream bigger, Eliza Mae. In America, you can own your own pastry shop if you so desire, instead of just working in one." Meghan pointed this out as she removed the day dress she was wearing. She went to the sink in her slip and under garments to freshen up before supper.

The look that crossed Eliza Mae's face was priceless. As she grasped hold of the truth of Meghan's words, surprise, elation, and a new found determination made her square her shoulders and hold her head a little higher. With hope-filled eyes she exclaimed, "I can own me own shop, can't I?"

In unison we answered, "Yes, ye can!" Then we all busted out laughing.

After our laughter quieted down, Eliza Mae marveled, "I never once thought of owning me own shop. It just never entered the imagination. Back home a woman owning her own business is very rare. I was planning on being content working for someone else but no more. Me goal now is ta be a business owner. I will have people working for me."

Meghan cheered, "Hurray, for free enterprise! Three cheers for America, the land of sweet opportunity and dreams that come true."

"Hip, Hip, Hurray! Hip, Hip, Hurray! Hip, Hip, Hooray!" we all cheered then once more dissolved into fits of laughter.

"I can just see it now," I exclaimed, spreading my hands to display a sign, "Eliza Mae's Tasty Treats!"

Janice shook her head, "No it should be, 'Eliza Mae's Devine Cakes and Pastries."

"Or how about, "Heaven on Earth Baked Goods!" chimed in Meghan.

Laughing, we kept it up until we noticed tears streaming down Eliza Mae's cheeks. A slightly sad smile played on her lips as she looked at us.

"What's the matter? " I asked, worried we had distressed her somehow. "This is supposed ta be fun. Yer not supposed ta be crying."

Eliza Mae closed her eyes for a moment, and we watched as large tears made wet paths down her cheeks only to drop onto the hands folded in her lap. Opening her eyes, she smiled, "Ye have no idea how much this all means ta me. Ye three have given me so much hope these last few days but most especially taday. I have been so forlorn since the death of me family that I could not see past me grief. Ye have opened me eyes ta the fact that there is still a plan and where there is hope there is life. I just want ta thank ye all for this." She sniffled, wiping her eyes.

There was no longer a dry eye in the room as we sandwiched Eliza Mae in a gigantic hug.

Meghan pulled away first from our hug wiping at the tears in her eyes. Looking into the mirror she gasped, "Well aren't we a sight, with our faces all blotchy and red."

Crowding around the mirror, we laughed and agreed with Meghan as we wiped at our tears. Hoping to remove any signs of our emotional afternoon, we soaked washcloths in cold water and then rested for a half of an hour with the cool damp material draped over our faces. All the while I laid there I was daydreaming about the glowing possibilities awaiting me in America.

Chapter 4

A little before six o'clock, refreshed and dressed, we made our way to the third class dining room for our evening supper. The dining area was quite large, seating a little over 450 people. White linen tablecloths and napkins adorned the rectangular tables, which were set to accommodate twenty people. The four of us made our way to a center table that was empty. Meghan and Eliza Mae sat across from Janice and me.

On the menu for Sunday was boiled corned beef served with carrots, cabbage, rutabagas, pearl onions, potatoes, and fresh baked bread. Butter, salt, pepper, and cider vinegar were the condiments available on our table, and water, milk, tea, or coffee was the beverage choices. Everything looked and smelled appetizing. After giving thanks for our food and asking God to bless those who prepared and served it, I eagerly sampled the fare finding it extremely delicious.

Quietly chatting amongst ourselves as we ate, we attempted to figure out where some of the people sitting near us were from by accents. For several it was easy but to some of the others who spoke different languages it was puzzlement. Smiles came readily enough when people noticed us glancing in their direction. It looked as if others too were passing the time as we were, in trying to figure out people's origin.

As our plates were cleared from the table, cottage pudding covered with a thick chocolate sauce, was served for dessert. It was certainly appealing to the palate and a gratifying end to a scrumptious meal.

Later, sipping coffee and enjoying the hum of activity in the crowded dining room, Janice leaned over to me and whispered, "I thought that we might see Amos in here this evening."

Wiping my fingertips on the napkin folded in my lap, I sighed, "Yes, I was kind of expecting to, but it seems that he must have eaten at an earlier sitting.

Meghan leaned forward seated on the edge of her chair, "Are you two discussing that man, Amos?"

Janice nodded her head, and Meghan continued, "Perhaps we will see him up in the General Room. I heard that there is going to be music and dancing there this evening. Maybe Shanna Kathryn will get another chance to dance with the gentleman again." she teased.

Eliza Mae giggled and glanced at me, "We can only hope, right Shanna Kathryn?"

I blushed embarrassed; not only by their teasing remarks but also at the uncanny way they had all struck on the same truth. I had been wishing for another chance to be close to the handsome young man. I just did not realize how much, until now.

Eliza Mae pushed her chair back away from the table and stood. "Let's go have a look in the General Room and see if anything is going on. We're finished here."

Suddenly, I was nervous at the possibility of running into Amos again. As we made ready to leave the table, my mind was racing with "what-ifs". "What if he has a girlfriend or worse yet, is married? What if he danced with many girls today and does not remember me as being one of them? What if he does remember but does not acknowledge me when we see each other. What if he is attracted to...?"

"Shanna Kathryn?" inquired Janice, shaking my arm to get my attention. "Are ye all right? I asked ye a question three times and ye just kept looking off inta space and then ye got a pained look about ye."

Feeling awkward, I stammered, "I'm all right. Me mind was taking me on a journey. I'm glad ye snapped me out of it." Then noticing that Meghan and Eliza Mae were not around, I asked. "Where are the others?"

Surprised at my question, Janice shook her head. "Ye must have really gone some place. They excused themselves ta go ta the restroom as soon as we left the table. They said they would meet us in the General Room."

Heat flooded my cheeks and my head throbbed. How awkward. I was so engrossed in my musings that I did not see the others leave.

Shrugging my shoulders, I smiled, "I was just thinking about Amos and what I would do if by chance he did not remember me."

Janice grinned and gestured with her hand, "Go on now. Him not remember a fine lass such as yerself? I don't think so! More like, he is avoiding ye, thinking ye wouldn't remember him."

Pacified, I grabbed Janice's hand. "Thank ye so much. I needed that."

She squeezed my hand and gave my arm a pat. "That, my dear is what friends are for. Now let us be going upstairs and see what kind of dancing they be doing. I know that I am up for a good old Irish jig, how about it?"

Laughing, we embraced and locking arms we quickly made our way up to the General Room where "Lannigan's Ball" was in full swing. Janice squealed in delight, dragging me with her onto the dance floor. In step with the others we danced merrily about the room laughing, and thrilled to be there, and sharing in the moment.

When the dance ended, cheers and requests for the "Kesh Jig" filled the place. "Hurrahs," sounded out when the first strains of the jig floated through the air from a pair of lads playing penny whistles. A young fellow quickly accompanied the two on the piano, while another kept beat on a drum like instrument called bodhran. Joining them on a fiddle, tickling our ears with his throaty strings was a graying hair, older man with twinkling blue eyes. His grin was infectious and he gave a loud "Woo hoo!" as another chap gave wind to the bagpipes.

To the Irish folk in the group, the music was sweet to the soul as well as to the feet. Young and old alike danced to the long-standing favorite, and I felt my heart swell within me. As I looked around the room at all the happy, smiling faces, I thought to myself, life was good. A prayer came to my lips just as Eliza Mae and Meghan joined in the dance. "Lord, never let me forget this moment as long as I live."

Reeling about the room, I felt something register deep within and I knew, without a shadow of doubt, that this moment had been chronicled in the inner recesses of my soul. It was stored away to that special place inside, where happy moments linger, waiting to resurface right when we need them most.

My eyes glistened with unshed tears, and I was sure that my whole heart was showing on my face as it radiated the joy I knew.

For a few seconds, sound disappeared as we spun about the room and suddenly I was seeing every person there with different eyes. In particular, there was an older couple across the room from me, obviously in love. They were holding hands as they danced, staring intently into each other's eyes. Their faces glowed with the light of their love and I could not take my eyes off them. It was a bittersweet moment for me, one that I can hardly explain. It just struck me that I was seeing something special and precious in their love. Tears burned in my eyes as I watched them and I felt to utter a little prayer for that love. "Father, I pray that Yer love will sustain their love always."

In saying this, sound returned and the couple disappeared from my view as dancers seemed to converge around them. My heart pounded in my chest and I had to get some air. Smiling and mouthing to Janice that I would be right back, I made my way to the door and then exited just as the tune, "Irish Washerwoman" began on the fiddle.

Chapter 5

Walking to the railing of the 3rd class promenade, I closed my eyes and took a deep breath. The crisp night air felt good and refreshing as it made its way into my lungs. Opening my eyes, I scanned the heavens. There were a few clouds floating in the moonless sky, but for the most part, the night was extremely clear. The stars loomed bright in the cosmos and appeared close enough to touch.

"They are beautiful aren't they?" inquired a familiar brogue from behind.

My heart thundered in my chest and my hands gripped the railing. Every fiber in my body was screaming in silent delight, 'Amos!'

Aloud, I murmured, "Yes they are."

Leaning with his back and elbows resting against the railing to my left, he turned his head toward me. I did not look in his direction immediately but watched him guardedly out of the corner of my eye. Clad in the same clothes he had on earlier, but now sporting a black wool jacket, I found him quite dashing with the collar flipped up around his neck to break the breeze. He certainly was a mighty fine looking man, and I could not help but smile at the thought of him standing next to me. To my chagrin, I watched a huge grin spread across his face, and I felt my own redden in shame at having my thoughts perceived. Trying to save face, I pushed away from the railing and confronted him with a scowl, "What are ye grinning about might I ask?"

His blue eyes sparkled as he replied shaking his head, "I'm grinning about ye, me dear lass."

"Me? What have I done ta cause ye such mirth?"

"Ye were trying to appear uninterested while ye were secretly inspecting me, and I found it amusing is all."

Placing my hands on my hips I quipped, "Well, I can see that ye are certainly full of yerself."

He puffed out his chest and lowered his brogue, "Only when I've such a fair colleen as yerself, looking me over am I full of meself."

The handsome smirk on his face assured me that He was savoring this conversation; in fact, I felt he was enjoying it a little too much, so I bit my tongue hoping to keep it from falling into another verbal trap with him.

Exasperated, I returned to the railing next to him and peered out into the large expanse of calm, dark water that reflected the stars above in its surface. His declaration of finding me fair kept going through my thoughts and a smile creased my lips as I realized I was enjoying myself in his company. All day long, I had been hoping to see him and now here he was, and I was acting like such a goose.

Turning toward him, my breath caught in my throat. He had also turned and was now a mere six inches from me. Looking up into his handsome face, I felt my heart skip a beat when he leaned forward and tenderly brushed a kiss upon my forehead.

Before I could think about what I was doing, my hand reached up to touch the place he had kissed. Dazed, by what had taken place, I just stood there looking up into his smiling face. "What was that for?"

"That my dear was because yer such a special young woman and I felt ta do so." Then he pulled my wrap closely about me and changed the subject.

"I saw ye and yer friends dancing in there," he said as he gestured with his head toward the General Room. "It appeared ta me that ye were having quite a good time."

Still a bit undone by his kiss and his nearness, I nodded my head. "We were having a good time, so much that I needed ta take break and catch me a breath."

Smiling, he turned to look out over the ocean. I joined him at the railing as he pointed to the sky and said, "He counts the number of the stars; He calls them all by name."

Recognizing Psalm 147, verse four, I looked heavenward at the billions of stars twinkling in the darkness. Suddenly I felt overwhelmed at the idea of knowing each by name. It was inconceivable to me. Glancing around, I began to notice the many people milling about enjoying the evening. Wonder dawned in me as I realized that God knew each one of those people by name. Though, strangers to me, He knew them and all their secret thoughts, hopes, dreams, and fears. I trembled at this revelation.

It appeared that Amos was thinking along the same line because when I looked up at him he was staring at me, his gaze penetrating into mine.

"Do ye know how infinite God is? Do ye not comprehend the height, depth, or width of His love for ye or any other? Just as those stars in the heavens are numbered so too are the very hairs of yer head. Do ye know that not one sparrow falls ta the ground apart from the Father's will? Not one! Do ye also know that yer of more value than a sparrow?"

Tears filled my eyes as I stared into the intense blue gaze of this handsome man who had ended his dialogue in a whisper. My heart felt like it was in my throat, and I did not know whether to swallow or weep at the beauty of what he had just shared. For the first time in my life, I was speechless.

Chapter 6

Taking my hand and placing it in the crook of his arm, he said, "Let's walk a bit."

Without hesitation, I let him guide me away from the railing. There were so many questions rolling around in my mind that I did not pay particular attention to where he was leading me. Only after we had stopped, did I notice that we were standing on the poop deck. I wasn't even aware of walking up the stairs to get here. Looking about I saw that, except for two couples leaning against the railing talking quietly, Amos and I were very much alone.

Removing my hand from his arm, I turned and faced him.

"Amos, there are so many questions I have for ye. It seems so strange ta say this, but it is as if I have known ye all me life and I know that is impossible. I know nothing about ye, yet I am sensing in me spirit that I do. Can ye understand what I mean?"

Taking my hand in his strong warm one he said, "Shall we sit?"

Nodding yes, he led me to a bench and we sat down. Still holding my hand he squeezed it and whispered, "Ask away."

My thoughts started running in many directions at once and I could not seem to focus on any one question in particular. Finally, I blurted out, "How did ye know me name? I don't remember Janice mentioning it when we danced taday. Yet when we parted, ye had whispered it."

He looked past me, for but a moment, and then his smiling eyes locked with my questioning ones. "We've met before."

"No." I said. "I would have remembered meeting ye. I am quite sure that we have never met before."

"Ye were a lot younger then, an impetuous teen on a wild adventure."

Frowning, I could not recall a time of ever meeting him. I would never have forgotten him; he was unforgettable. An idea came to mind, "Are ye a friend of me brother? Is that how ye

19

know me?"

"That is not how I know ye."

"Ugh." Annoyed I buried my face in my free hand and massaged my temples.

"Shanna Kathryn."

Moving my hand to the side of my face, I focused my attention on him and he continued.

"I will give ye time ta think about our meeting and if ye cannot remember before this journey ends, I will share with ye the location. Agreed?"

What more could I do? I did not remember him.

"Agreed, but I don't think it's very fair of ye, ta be keeping it a secret."

"Humph, I think I should be the one doing the complaining because ye have greatly wounded me manliness by not remembering me."

Rolling my eyes, I patted the side of his cheek and quipped, "There ye go again getting all full of yerself. Perhaps that is the reason I forgot ye in the first place. I never thought too highly of a man whose conceit outshines his wit."

"Ouch! That hurt! I think I'd better get ye back to yer friends before ye say anything else that would maim me finely tuned opinion of meself."

His 'Woe is me' facial expression caused laughter to bubble up inside of me. "Finely tuned indeed, Sir, have ye no shame or have ye always been this vain?"

"Look here, yer getting a bit unreasonable don't ye think? Me? Vain? Never!"

"Never?' I asked with a raised brow.

Smirking, he gave me a crooked smile, "Well, perhaps on occasion, but enough of this picking on me, what is yer next question."

The words rolled off my lips before I even I had time to think. "How is it that ye know so much of the Word of God?"

Surprise registered on his face. I had clearly caught him off guard. "Well now, that is about as far away from the topic we were on as the green shores of Ireland are from this vessel."

"Well I hope ye answer this question because the first one, in me opinion, went unanswered."

His brows rose over his eyes, "Ye are quite the contentious little creature aren't ye?"

"Ugh, yer still avoiding me question!" I stated.

Amos shrugged his shoulders with a grin on his face. "I know so much of the Word of God because..."

He stopped here, and leaned forward, as if he was going to tell me a secret. I leaned toward him because I wanted to hear clearly, what he was going to say.

"I know the Word of God." He whispered, smiled and, sat back.

Sighing, my chin dropped to my chest and I covered my eyes with my hand. "So yer saying, that ye read the Bible and have memorized it or are ye a minister or something?" I looked up piercing him with a questioning stare.

His grin broadened, he shrugged and let go of my hand to fold his arms smugly across his chest. "Ye could say the something."

Exasperated, I growled, "Amos, yer not answering me questions. These answers are wild goose chases. Now answer me!"

"Me dear, Shanna Kathryn, I have answered yer questions, ye just dinna like the answers."

Jumping up, I paced the deck in front of him. The man was insufferable! Casting a quick glance in his direction, made my cheeks redden in annoyance. He was just sitting there, grinning like a mindless half-wit, and it took everything I had to control my impulse of wanting to punch him in the nose.

"Are ye married?" flew off my tongue, before I could think about what I was asking. I was pleased to see the triumphant smile leave his face, but I was chagrined to watch his whole countenance darken. Shaking his head he stood, towering over me with his hands clenched at his sides.

"Ye shame me lass!" He said irate. "Do ye think it would be proper for me ta be spending time with ye if'n I was married? I tell ye, I wouldn't! Ye, Miss Shanna Kathryn, are certainly a poor judge of character. What ye are suggesting is evil, and we are told ta abstain from appearances of evil."

Shamefaced at my bad manners and wrong assumptions, I apologized. "Oh Amos, please forgive me for blundering so badly. I am sorry, both that I have offended ye, and that I let me own insecurities rule me tongue. It's a fault I need very much ta amend."

He looked at me quietly for a few moments, as if contemplating the sincerity of my words, and then his countenance changed, and I cannot help but think that he was somehow, pleased by the admission of my weakness.

My heart skipped a beat when he smiled that dazzling smile and graciously announced, "Yer forgiven. Now let us talk about these insecurities. What's the cause of that, might I ask?"

Chapter 7

Returning to the bench, I sat down and waited for him to again be seated next to me. Shrugging my shoulders and staring up into the star filled night, I began to tell him my story.

"I was only three when me Da left us. I can still remember it like it just happened. Da, me older sister, brother, and meself were sitting around the table eating boiled potatoes and lamb for supper. Mum sat in a rocker near the fire place, nursing me baby sister as the two of them bickered across the room, like they always did, over money, and the lack of it, when suddenly, me Da jumped up from his chair screaming that he couldn't take it any longer, and he was leaving us. And just like that, he left."

I nibbled at my bottom lip, fighting back tears that the memory caused. Looking down into my clasped hands, I went on. "As he headed out the door, he told me Mum, who was crying now and begging him to stay, that he would send us money when he could, and with only the clothes on his back, he walked out of our lives forever."

I looked at Amos who was watching me closely and said in a whisper. "I have never been able to eat lamb again, peculiar, huh?"

Shaking his head no, Amos said, "Go on with yer story."

"Well, If not for me Mum's family coming alongside us and helping us out, I believe that we might have had ta be split up, ye know, ta be fostered out ta other families ta be raised. As hard and scary as it already was, that would have been awful ta lose me Mum and siblings too. With the help of our grandparents, we were able ta keep our small cottage, but me Mum had ta go ta work so that left us four children on our own for much of the time, taking up the slack that me Da's leaving had caused."

Swiping angrily at a tear in the corner of my eye, I sniffed. "It was a scary time for us. I remember on more than one occasion being left alone for hours upon hours. Me Mum went ta work as a laundress, which kept her away from home much of the day and sometimes the night. I would lie abed fearful and afraid that she would not return. I guess I believed, deep down, that she would also leave. Countless times I lay awake, with me heart pounding in me ears, desperately waiting for the sound of her arrival."

Pausing in my narrative, I smiled at Amos, "And by the grace of God she always came home. As I grew older, the fear of being abandoned was not as prevalent, but it was still there so I began ta read in the evenings ta take me mind off of the fact that me Mum was working. It was during this time that I developed an avid obsession for books. I have read the Bible at least a dozen or so times from cover ta cover, as well as any book that had ta do with adventure. Actually, anything that I could get me hands upon was fair game. So there ye have it, me life story in a nutshell, ye might say."

Amos was staring up at nothing in particular as I ended my discourse. For a moment, I thought that he had not heard me, and then he asked, "So what is taking ye ta America?"

"Me Mum's brother, me uncle and his family, settled there years ago. The linen factory, where I worked, is not the safest place of employment, and they have wanted me ta come stay, so they secured me passage on the Titanic. Once I have settled in there, I will look for work, hopefully finding a position that suits me."

He was looking at me now and his stare was piercing, "Do ye know the scripture in Joshua chapter 1 where God tells Joshua, after the death of Moses, that he is ta lead the Israelites over the Jordan River and inta the Promise Land? God says in verse five that, 'There shall not any man be able to stand before thee all the days of thy life: as I was with Moses, so I will be with thee: I will not fail thee nor forsake thee.' And further down in verse nine He again tells Joshua, 'Have I not commanded thee? Be strong and of good courage; be not afraid, neither be thou dismayed: for the Lord thy God is with thee whithersoever thou goest.' Are ye familiar with that passage?"

I nodded my head as my nose started to burn inside from the tears that were forming in my eyes. I knew what he was alluding to. He wanted me to know the truth that even though me Da had left us, we had never been alone. The Creator of Heaven and Earth had never failed us, even when things seemed their bleakest. Looking back, I could see that now, but at the time of living through it, that fact was not so obvious.

As if reading my thoughts Amos whispered, "It may not have been apparent, but it was nonetheless real. He never left ye and He never will."

Wiping at the now falling tears, I smiled, "It seems like all I've done taday is cry. I don't know what is the matter with me?"

Taking a handkerchief from inside his coat, Amos placed it in my hand. Smiling my thanks, I dabbed at my cheeks, took a deep breath, and sat back. Tilting my head, I gazed up at the heavens above that were now crystal clear. Twinkling stars appeared as diamonds against black velvet, and the thought of God placing each one there with His finger overwhelmed me. My eyes stung with fresh tears at the enormity that we are never alone. Taking another deep breath, I realized in awe that He was the very air I was breathing and this revelation caused me to shudder and gasp. All those nights I was so terrified of being alone and fearful of me Mum not returning, He had been there with me and my siblings. Years of fear, shame, and insecurity broke away from my heart where I had been holding them close for so long. I felt empty and vulnerable all at once, and the hurt of those past years poured forth from the depth of my being. The dam that had been holding back the floodgates burst and I lost myself to nonstop sobbing. Amos reached for me with tender hands, and held me in his strong arms soothing me with soft words as he rubbed my back.

I do not know how long I cried. I just know that when I thought I was finished and began gulping down air to try and quiet myself, I would remember I was breathing Him in and the whole thing started all over again.

It was a humbling process to be sure. I had soaked the shoulder area of Amos's coat with tears and I was mortified, but I could not seem to stop. He was so good through it all.

Finally, when the well of tears seemed to have dried up, I pulled out of his embrace, in much embarrassment, and blew my nose loudly in his handkerchief. Trying to achieve some order of semblance to myself, I patted my hair, straightened my wrap, and inhaled strong determination before turning toward him. The moment I met his caring eyes I knew the well was refilling.

"Shanna Kathryn, we are not finished here yet. There is one last thing that needs ta be done, and that is, ye must forgive yer Da."

Chapter 8

I had read the Bible many times and every time I came to the New Testament and the gospels where Jesus tells us that unless we forgive others He cannot forgive us, I would quickly read over those parts, rationalizing that He was not talking to me. 'Surely, He cannot expect me to forgive me Da for leaving us. He is talking about something else.' Within myself, I knew the truth, but I couldn't forgive him for all the pain he had caused us. I could not and would not!

Shaking my head at Amos I replied, "Ye ask too much. How can I forget all that he has done?"

"It is impossible, ta ask ye ta forget all that ye went through, but that is not what He desires of ye. What ye went through has made ye inta who ye are taday. No, He just wants ye ta forgive him."

Confused, I shook my head, "I don't understand. Isn't forgiving forgetting all that has been done? Does not God say that, 'I will forgive their iniquity, and I will remember their sin no more'? Perhaps, He can do so because He is God, but I am not, and I will not forgive nor forget!"

I would not look at Amos, but stared stonily ahead, relishing the fact that it was my due to hate me Da! It was my right because of what he put me through! I will not forgive him! I will not!

Amos responded to my outburst in a soft voice. "Many have confused the meaning about what Jesus was saying when He told us ta forgive and ye will be forgiven. Forgive means to send away or dismiss. So when someone wrongs us, and we hold that wrong within us we are the ones that reap the bondage, guilt, and hurt of the wrong done. God cannot deal with the person who wronged us because we are holding onta their sin. We have made them indebted ta us by our unforgiveness and, essentially, we have set ourselves up as their judge, and we are warned that when we judge we ourselves will be judged. Someone will have ta be dealt with over the sin committed and since yer holding onta it, guess who gets to deal with it? We must send their sin back ta them by forgiving them. This opens the door for God ta now move, and deal with the area in their life where they have hurt others. That is why ye can see someone who wronged ye just as happy as a lark, and going about their own merry way, while ye are still fuming over what they done ta ye."

Unwilling to give an inch just yet, I felt myself squirm under the pressure of what this new revelation meant to me. My un-forgiveness had been part of my life for so long, and I did not honestly think that I was ready to part with it.

"So yer saying, that I don't have ta forget what he has done, but I need ta forgive him for what he's done?" I still would not look at Amos.

"When ye forgive ya dunna lose the memory, but I will tell ya that when ye forgive, the memory can be replaced by something else. Shanna Kathryn, forgiveness is for us. It severs the chord that ties us ta the other. We put conditions on our forgiveness like, when they feel as bad as I do, I'll forgive them, but that's not what it means ta forgive. The ability ta forgive is truly a blessing in yer life. Send his sin away from ye freeing yerself and thus allowing God ta work on him. It's the only way lass. It's the only way."

My heart felt like it was ready to explode in my chest and my head was throbbing. I felt confused and hopeful at the same time, and it was tearing me up. Wringing my hands in my lap I turned to him, "Amos I don't even know if he's dead or alive. How can forgiveness help me if he's dead?"

Touching my cheek tenderly with his finger, he whispered, "It helps ye. Send the sin away from ye and forgive him."

Tears were streaming down my cheeks as I looked up into his compelling blue eyes. Sniffling, my head dropped forward, and I inquired, "How?"

It seemed that he was waiting for that question, "Just repeat after me, Father, I forgive me Da. Please forgive me for holding unforgiveness in me heart all these years. I release him, wherever he is to Ye. Forgive me for judging him, and please release me from reaping that same judgment in me own life. Thank Ye, Lord. Amen."

As I repeated after him, something warm pierced my heart, and some of the pain and anger I had stored there for years toward me Da seemed to pass away to some extent. Amos's next words continued the matter.

"Do ye know that hurt people, hurt people, Shanna Kathryn? Yer father's leaving and the subsequent hurting of ye children, was because he was already a hurt individual inside, and there was no one ta teach him any different. One of yer grandparents must have been hurt, and in turn hurt yer Da, and yer Da hurt ye. If the vicious cycle does not stop, through forgiveness, ye too will hurt others. God will not be mocked, whatever a man sows he shall also reap. If ye plant potatoes, do ye get carrots?"

At the shaking of my head, he agreed, "That's correct. If I plant potatoes, I get potatoes. If I sow kindness, I reap kindness, and if I sow love, love is what I will get in return. The same goes for things of a negative nature, if I sow unforgiveness, that is exactly what I will have in me life. It's a law that has been in effect since the beginning of time and there is no getting around it. Ye just have ta change what yer sowing."

Still sniffling, I smiled and dabbed at my eyes and nose with his handkerchief. My head and neck were throbbing from the tension of the last few minutes, so I inhaled deeply trying to help the pain dissipate, but it had no effect. Amos placed his hands upon my shoulders and told me to turn so that he could massage the ache in my neck. I did as requested, and felt his strong hands grip, squeeze, and rub the strain of the evening away. He silently kept this up for a few minutes and when he spoke again, he had changed the subject.

"Shanna Kathryn, what an interesting name ye have. Shanna is a good Irish name meaning lovely, while Kathryn is English and means powerful and pure. Hmm, yer name literally means beauty that is moving and unspoiled."

My hand covered my mouth, and my eyes closed as I fought back tears again. Swallowing hard I gulped down air, trying to still the tempo of my racing heart. A memory from my childhood came to me; I was three years old and in our cottage, and me Mum was brushing my hair. As she ministered to me in this fashion, she began telling me about the day I was born.

Me Da had come in from working the potato fields to find the midwife just leaving, and congratulating him on the blessing of having a fine healthy daughter. He came to where me Mum laid in their bed, nursing the new dark haired addition to their family. Me Mum had told me, that me Da had taken one look at me, and said I was one of the most beautiful little girls he had ever seen. He took me in his arms and snuggled me close stating that I was indeed 'beauty unspoiled'. That was how I came to be called Shanna Kathryn. Suddenly, I knew that me Da had loved me and my siblings, but he was just too wrapped up in his own wounds to see the hurt he would cause us by walking away. He could not have been happy to leave us. It must have been miserable for him, knowing that he left four children fatherless, and in a twinkling I began to see me Da in a whole new light. Whereas before, I had always imagined him living happily with a whole new family, I now saw him as a man who was probably haunted by what he had done. Suddenly, all the anger and hatred I had felt toward him for so long turned to pity and regret. Silently, I asked God to bless him, wherever he was, and I knew that the healing process in my life had begun. I looked forward to sharing this liberating counsel with the rest of my family.

I did not communicate any of this revelation with Amos, but I had a feeling that he knew because he gave my shoulders a final squeeze and then stood up.

"Come lass, let us be getting ye back ta yer friends. This night air has a bite to it, and I would not have ye claiming that I kept ye out too long."

Rising to my feet with his assistance, I turned to him laying my hand upon his firm chest, and whispered, "Amos...I appreciate all that ye did for me this night."

He grabbed both my arms above my elbows and gave them a gentle squeeze, "It was me pleasure, Shanna Kathryn." Then taking my elbow he guided me along the deck back to the General Room where another tune was just beginning.

Looking hopefully at him, I stammered, "How 'bout another dance, kind sir?"

He smiled, looked past me into the lively room, and shook his head. "As much as I would love ta swing ye around and hold ye in me arms again, I must decline the invite. This cold has me chilled and I am going ta head ta me cabin for a spot of tea and scones."

Laughing, I teased, "That sounds a wee bit English of ye sir, and here I be thinking ye ta be a fine Irish lad! What will me Mum say?"

"She will say, 'Now there be a laddie that has good taste in all areas of his life'."

Laughing heartily at his comment, I inquired, "Oh, would she now?"

"Most certainly, she would! As I'm a handsome lad with proper etiquette too, she will no doubt be extolling me virtues to all her friends. 'Why he has such charisma and charm, Shanna Kathryn was swept off her feet, by the likes of him'."

"Oh ho ho. . . really?" I chortled. "I must conclude sir that the night air has certainly gone ta yer head. So off to bed with ye now, as there are tea and scones awaiting yer pompous appetite."

"Pompous! Are ye calling me pompous?"

"If the shoe fits laddie..."

"Well. . .I. . . well. . . I guess it was kind of a pompous remark, wasn't it?" he asked sheepishly.

Nodding my head and grinning, I smacked his cheek tenderly saying, "Just a wee bit."

Turning toward the gangway he smiled, "I enjoyed meself tonight, Shanna Kathryn, and I hope ye did too."

"I did Amos, more than ye can ever know. Will I see ye tomorrow?"

Amos stopped and looked up at the starry hosts before turning to grin at me. "Yes ye will be seeing me. Now, don't ye be staying up too late, as yer going ta be needing yer rest. And don't ye forget ta try and remember where we have met." Striving to look forlorn, he continued, "Because me vain opinion of meself, still suffers over that one."

Giggling, I bit my lower lip then said, "I shall try ta remember, but do not forget that if I can not, ye have ta be telling me."

"I will tell ye, dunna ye fret Shanna Kathryn, now sweet sleep, me dear." he said softly, waving at me before disappearing through the door.

Chapter 9

Janice appeared at my side, "Was that Amos I just saw ye talking to?"

"Yes, and, Janice, I have so much to tell ye and the others. Come, let us go dance some more, or have ye had yer fill?"

She smiled, "I can have another go at it if ye want ta dance. I was just worried about ye when ye did not return, so I came ta see what became of ye."

Linking our arms together, we ran toward the revelry and jumped into the merriment with the rest. Eliza Mae and Meghan both shrieked when they saw us, and we all grabbed each other's hands and twirled to the music. It was a jovial time; one that still lingers on in the recesses of my mind.

Everything seemed notably more vivid; colors, sounds, scents, and my emotions just seemed . . . so receptive! I cannot explain it any better than to say that such peace flooded my soul that I felt truly alive for the first time. I was aware of a change deep within; wholeness, like I had never experienced before, and it was extremely gratifying.

With the ending of the song, giggling, we all fell into one another and made the decision to head back to our cabin. Laughter and happy chatter followed us all the way there, and I could not wait to share all that had happened earlier this evening with them. My forgiving me Da was such a freeing matter that I wanted them to know about it. As we took turns at the sink preparing for bed, I filled them in on most of what had occurred with my visit with Amos. There was not a dry eye in the cabin once I completed my narration, and Meghan admitted that there were a couple people in her life that, she too, needed to forgive. She said that she would work on that area of her life and see what comes about.

It was about 10:00 P.M. when we all crawled into our bunks for the night. Janice grabbed a book of poetry to read, Meghan did some cross stitch, while Eliza Mae just pulled her covers high over head, to get some sleep.

As it is my habit to read a Psalm before falling asleep each night, I grabbed my Bible and opened to this evenings reading; Psalm 46.

"God is our refuge and strength, a very present help in trouble. Therefore will not we fear, though the earth be removed, and though the mountains be carried into the midst of the sea; Though the waters thereof roar and be troubled, though the mountains shake with the swelling thereof. Selah.

There is a river, the streams whereof shall make glad the city of God, the holy place of the tabernacles of the most High. God is in the midst of her; she shall not be moved: God shall help her, and that right early. The heathen raged, the kingdoms were moved: he uttered his voice, the earth melted. The LORD of hosts is with us; the God of Jacob is our refuge. Selah.

Come, behold the works of the LORD, what desolations he hath made in the earth. He maketh wars to cease unto the end of the earth; he breaketh the bow, and cutteth the spear in sunder; he burneth the chariot in the fire. Be still, and know that I am God: I will be exalted among the heathen; I will be exalted in the earth. The LORD of hosts is with us; the God of Jacob is our refuge. Selah."

As I finished reading this passage of eleven verses a shiver ran through my body and I felt apprehensive, but I did not know why. I re-read the Psalm, but could not understand what it was that made me feel nervous. Silently, I inquired, "What is going on Lord?"

And like a whisper inside my head, I heard, "Fear not. I will never leave you nor forsake you." Instantly peace flooded my soul.

I put the Bible aside and snuggled under the covers, confident of that promise. My last thoughts, before falling asleep, were of Amos's handsome face, and startling blue eyes.

Chapter 10

"Shanna Kathryn!"

Rolling over in my bunk, I put my pillow over my head to drown out whoever was calling my name. It couldn't possibly be time to get up already; it seemed that I had only just fallen asleep.

"Shanna Kathryn hurry, get up!"

Suddenly, I was wide awake and sitting up in my bunk. The cabin was dark, but a sliver of light could be seen coming in under the door.

'Why am I up?' I wondered. At that moment a sharp knock came upon our cabin door.

"Shanna Kathryn, wake up!" came the urgent plea.

'That's Amos!' I thought. Climbing out of the bunk and grabbing my robe, I cinched it at the waist, before leaning against the portal and whispering, "Is that ye, Amos?"

"Yes it is! I need ta speak with ye immediately."

Hesitating for only a moment, I opened the door and there he was looking every bit as handsome as I remembered him. Glancing at me and taking in my disheveled appearance he grinned, but hastily said, "I didn't think I was ever going ta wake ye."

Crossing my arms in front of me, and trying to put some semblance of order to my hair, I smiled, "Well ye did. Now what was so important that ye couldn't wait till morning, ta tell me?"

He peered down the hallway in both directions before turning an intense gaze upon me. Something about his manner put me on edge and I felt the unease I had sensed earlier, after reading my psalm, return. "Do ye trust me?" he asked.

Goose flesh spread over me at the intensity of his voice, but I knew that after today, I would trust him always. "Yes Amos, I trust ye."

His tone was grave, "I want ye ta do something for me. I want ye ta wake the others and then I would like ye all ta dress in yer warmest things. If ye have any money or valuables that can be carried in a pocket, bring them, otherwise leave all behind. Once ye have your coats on, put yer life belts that are in yer cabin on, and then meet me out here. I will then escort ye ta the deck."

My heart was thundering in my chest and the apprehension I had been feeling, came funneling in around me. Wide-eyed and scared, I reached for Amos's arms and clung to them, "Why Amos? What is going on?"

He was so solemn and I noticed that his sparkling blue eyes were dark, and though I could not read what was in them, I sensed he had something very serious to tell me.

"A moment ago, the Titanic hit an iceberg, and she is going down fast. In a few minutes the crew will receive the orders ta uncover the lifeboats, and we have ta be on our way before then. Ye must hurry and wake the others."

Dumbfounded, I inquired, "What time is it?"

Turning me about and shoving me back into the cabin, he whispered. "It's 11:42 p.m. Now hurry, I will wait right here for ye!" And then he shut the door behind me.

Standing in the dark, I was stunned at the enormity of what was taking place. My mind screamed, 'Oh Lord, this cannot be happening!' I wanted to cry, but I couldn't. All at once, verse one of the psalm I had read earlier came to me, "God is our refuge and strength; a very present help in trouble."

Peace halted my trembling as I realized that God had primed me for this moment when He had shared His psalm with me. Strength and boldness propelled me into action. I turned on the light and straight away proclaimed, "Arise and shine ladies, our God will help us and preserve us this day!"

Janice rolled over in her bunk and asked, "Arise and what?'

"Shine. I am sure she said shine." muttered Meghan as she flung an arm over her eyes, trying to block out the unwanted light.

Eliza Mae sat up yawning, "What is going on?"

I was already undressing, "Word has come that we are to dress in our warmest attire, and after putting on our coats, we must also don our life belts. It seems we have hit an iceberg and the ship is sinking."

Three sets of horrified eyes stared at me as dawning of the pending disaster registered in their drowsy brains. I knew there was no time to waste. "Ladies we must hurry! Oh and I almost forgot, if ye have any money or valuables that can be slipped into yer pockets, bring them, otherwise everything else is ta remain."

Janice began to cry and fear shook her small body. She was immobile for a moment with trembling, so I went to her and put my arms around her, holding her close. "I cannot explain the why of it Janice, but I feel that if we do as we are instructed and keep calm, we will all come ta safety. Can ye trust me in this?"

She nodded wiping her eyes and nose on the sleeve of her nightgown. "Okay, ye need to be getting ready and quickly."

Meghan and Eliza Mae were both nearly dressed, but I could see the fear in their eyes. Reaching for them, I grabbed their hands and gave each a reassuring squeeze. "The Lord is our help and we will not fear, okay?" Both nodded in unison.

Turning, I finished gathering my warmest attire and minutes later, when we all stood arrayed in our coats and life belts, a soft knock beckoned us at the door.

"Amos!" exclaimed Janice, the moment the portal was opened.

"Ladies!" he commanded their attention with his curt tone. "We are on E deck which means we have ta traverse up five decks ta get ta the life boats. It is very, very important that ye obey me every word and follow me. No matter what ye see, hear, or think, ye are ta keep yer eyes fixed on me and do not look ta the left or ta the right, but follow me precisely, do ye understand?"

I nodded my head yes and watched as the three others looked at me and then did the same.

"Good. Now the first thing I want ye ta do is ta go, single file keeping ta the right side of every hallway we enter. Shanna

Kathryn is ta follow directly behind me, then Janice, Eliza Mae, and Meghan ye will bring up the rear."

Four faces stared aghast at him, and I blurted out, "How do ye know their names?"

"I promise to explain it all ta ye later but right now we must go." And without another word he led the way along the quiet corridor.

It seemed strange that there were not hundreds of people running about panic stricken, when it finally dawned on me, there had not been an official alarm raised yet. Everyone was still sleeping and had no idea that the ship was going down. Distraught, I cried out, "Amos! What about all the others? Who will see them ta safety?"

Amos did not slow down but kept up the fast pace he had started upon. "We must press on, Shanna Kathryn."

Reaching forward I grabbed his jacket, "Stop! We must wake the others!"

Amos turned and grabbed me by the shoulders, "Listen, I am only going ta explain this once! What is taking place now will be spoken about for years ta come. This is going ta be a horrible tragedy, and only a few will survive. The four of ye can endure, but only if ye listen ta me and obey. Is this understood?"

Tears coursed down my cheeks, "But..."

He cut me off, "There are no buts about it! We must go!" And then he turned and moved along the companionway.

Silently, I offered prayers heavenward for those who were still sleeping. I felt like I was suffocating in my despair, but I kept trailing after Amos.

"Wait!" shouted Amos in the silent hallway, startling me when he took off running toward the stairs. Not exactly sure about what to do, I turned and, looking at the other three girls whose eyes were wide and wild with terror, made the decision to run after him. My cabin mates followed and we reached the stairs in a panic, only to find two crew members in the process, of pulling a gate across the top of them.

Seeing us, they hesitate, look questioningly at each other,

glance behind themselves, and then quickly motioned to us. "Hurry ladies, you must hurry!" entreated the older of the two men as we climbed the stairs and passed through the gate. No sooner had Meghan's feet attained the new level, did they brush by her, closing and securing the structure with a lock.

In horror, Meghan stared at them aghast, "Why are you doing that? There are still hundreds of people down there. How are they supposed to get out if you are locking the gate?"

Stepping forward, the older man patted her arm, "It's okay lass, it's just a precautionary measure. We cannot have hundreds of people crowding around the lifeboats and fighting their way in. We have to handle this in an orderly manner. As soon as the first and second class passengers are all settled in we will open the gates for the others to get to their life boats. No need to fear, but you ladies must be on your way."

Thus dismissed, we hastened to catch up with Amos who had not stopped when we had. Without turning, he said gruffly over his shoulder, "Ye cannot stop like ye just did, no matter what. Every second we have is precious and going ta be needed ta get ye into a lifeboat. Are we clear on this?"

"Yes." I whimpered, closely behind him. My head ached, I felt nauseated, and there was a ringing in my ears, but all this could not drown out the new sounds that were taking place on the deck above us. I could hear shouts and the pounding of hurried steps along with doors opening and closing. I was frightened because it all sounded so chaotic.

From behind us, we could now hear people screaming, "For the love of God man, open this gate!" and then the gate was rattled to the point that I felt for sure that its hinges would be shaken out of the wall. I could imagine desperate hands pulling at the metal trying to rip it apart, but to no avail. Bile rose in my throat, and I prayed non-stop for God to have mercy. I could hear Janice repeat over and over, "Oh Sweet Jesus, Mary, and Joseph, save us!" Until her supplications were a litany with Meghan chiming in on the 'save us' part.

Everything was surreal, and I took a second to peek over my

shoulder to see how the others were faring, and what I saw in their countenance mirrored my own distress, I was sure. Pale and fearful they were with a haunted look about them. I could not abide gazing at them any longer, so I concentrated on Amos' sturdy muscular form leading the way, and the racing of my heart seemed to calm a little.

We turned the corner, and the hallway erupted with activity as men, women, and children loaded down with their belongings, hastened toward the staircase, which would take them to the deck above. People were pushing and shoving and, in horror, I watched as an elderly man was knocked to the floor and trampled upon by six men before someone helped him to his feet. Limping and in tears, the man slowly made his way to the group assembled at the base of the stairs.

Heavily laden with their earthly treasures, passengers struggled to put on their life belts while shoving their way to the stairs. We four, while doing our best to keep up with Amos, forced our way through the mass of people gathering at the stairway which was barricaded with a gate and two crew members standing guard. Amos walked on by and this action surprised me. I slowed my pace and called out to him, "Shouldn't we wait here ta go up with the others?"

Shaking his head, he commanded, "Just keep following me!"

Slowly now, because of the number of passengers milling about the aisle way, we made our way down the long corridor of D deck, passing another stairwell full of passengers bickering with the crewmen to open the gates. Many of those standing around the stairs were burdened down with baggage, and I remember thinking, 'Do they really believe that they'll be able to take that with them on the lifeboats?' Looking back on it now, I feel that my observation of this, as we ourselves walked empty handed toward the lifeboats, was insightful. We were leaving our baggage behind.

Amos finally turned left at the end of the corridor and then a quick right, leading us up the direct access ladders used by the crew. We did not come into contact with a single soul on those ladders. Relief overwhelmed me, for a moment, as we attained C Deck but it was short lived because I had assumed that Amos would continue on up the ladders to the next level, but he moved on in a forward direction instead.

All at once three crew members, who were hastening up the access ladders we had just abandoned, stopped their assent and called out to us. "Ladies, you're going the wrong way! Come along with us and we will get you to the Boat deck!"

Looking at Amos who had stopped and was looking at us and shaking his head, I hollered out to the three, "Thank ye kind sirs, but we are going ta continue on this way."

Snorting, one of the crew men stated belligerently, "If you keep going that way then, you're going to meet your Maker!"

Fear boiled in me at that statement, and I sensed that Amos realized this because he looked me straight in the eyes and remarked, "Remember; trust me."

I quickly glanced at the others to make sure we were all in agreement because for a brief moment, I was unsure whether or not to keep following Amos. What those sailors had said affected me more than I had thought, and I needed assurance from another that we were doing the right thing. All three girls shrugged their shoulders and nodded their heads in acquiescence to my unspoken question. Relief overwhelmed me therefore I rushed after Amos to close the gap that my indecision had made between us.

What happened next was so peculiar that for a moment, I had the thought that I was dreaming the entire event. As we persisted in moving forward past the Well Deck, we reached the 2nd Class entrance and, unlike the lower levels there seemed to be no hurry in anyone here. People were moving casually about sitting and talking. Nowhere did we see the anxiousness that was displayed below. It was as if they were totally oblivious to the danger that lay ahead of them, or perhaps they did know but since the Titanic was supposed to be practically unsinkable, they were of the opinion, 'why worry?' Waiters were even serving some of the guest libations, and this strange occurrence caused me to revaluate our trailing Amos. I began thinking that perhaps he had misjudged the whole affair, and things were not as dire as he had predicted. To top it all off, I could hear music being played somewhere and it was so odd to me because it seemed out of context to what was supposed to be happening. Looking at the other girls, I sensed that they too were experiencing the same peculiar thing.

My steps faltered for a moment as I viewed those around us who paid us no mind, looking as if they had not a care in the world. Then I recalled the scripture in Proverbs 14 that says, "There is a way which seemeth right unto a man, but the end thereof are the ways of death."

Remembering the locked gates below and the statements of the crewmen we had run into, I shook with fear for these people, and prayed silently for God to have mercy on them. My doubts ebbed, and I continued on the course that had been established earlier that evening, as I hurried to catch up to Amos.

He surprised me by cutting through the 2nd Class Library, which on a normal day and given the opportunity I would have loved to examine the extensive volume of books lining the shelves. As it was, my steps faltered and my pace slowed considerably as I traveled through the richly decorated room. Mahogany furniture placed around a beautiful Persian carpet pulled the area together giving it a warm comfy feeling. Silk curtains adorned the large windows, and I was saddened as we passed that way thinking that all this beauty could very well end up on the bottom of the ocean.

I struggled to believe that lives would be lost as I surmised that such a grand vessel as, the Titanic would have made the proper provisions to see to the safety of its passengers, so for the time, my thoughts were on the beauty of the things around me possibly being gone forever.

Our trek continued past the Aft 2nd Class stairway which is found at the back of the ship, to the Forward 2nd Class stairway where we ran into a snag. It appeared that many others on board had the same idea as we did and I half expected Amos to turn

43

around and go another way, but he remained where he was silently scanning the area with a look of determination etched upon his face. At that moment, the sky lit up with a distress rocket. On any other occasion, I would have commented on the beauty of the glittering sparks falling to the ocean surface, but instead, the four of us huddled together behind Amos wondering what would happen next. We did not have long to wait because he turned to us and whispered, "Take hold of the hand of the lass behind ye as we are gonna press our way through this throng of passengers all the way ta the Boat Deck."

Doing as we were instructed, I grabbed for Janice's hand, and she for Eliza Mae's, and Eliza Mae took hold of Meghan's hand, and we made a train of sorts. Amos seized my right hand maneuvering us to the right side of the stairwell all the time ascending one stair at a time. It was slow going and there were a few protests from those we urged out of the way in our passing, but for the most part, it was uneventful, and in a matter of time we were on the Boat Deck which turned out to be an extremely chaotic place.

Chapter 11

Though our journey from E Deck to the Boat Deck did not seem to take long, in actuality, the ascent was close to an hour. Four lifeboats had already been launched on the starboard side and three on the port side.

Gazing at the remaining boats, however, caused bile to rise up in my throat. I knew in that second that there was certainly not enough room in the remaining lifeboats to hold all the passengers still waiting in steerage and elsewhere.

Amos had been accurate when he had told me that only a few were going to survive this horror. It was inconceivable, but the Titanic was not properly prepared for a disaster such as this. This travesty was going to haunt many for years to come.

Looking up at Amos, who still held my hand and observing his grim countenance, tears stung in the corners of my eyes as I wailed, "No! No! No! This cannot be happening Amos! No!"

Squeezing my hand, he brought it to his lips for a quick kiss before leading us down the port side of the boat deck toward the stern. Here 1St Class passengers mingled with 2nd and 3rd Class passengers. Crew members were loading women and children into the boats first. It was horrible to see children clinging to their daddies crying, while their mommies tried dragging them away to get them safely into a boat. Several men attempted fearless demonstrations for their wives and children appearing composed and optimistic in the face of their distress but as their loved ones were lowered to the ocean below many sobbed in anguish, knowing there was little hope of surviving the night, and their fear and sorrow was etched upon their faces. A few even turned aside and eliminated the contents of their stomachs right there on the deck. The whole situation was too ghastly for words, and I closed my eyes for a moment trying to block their anguish from my sight, but I could not, knowing at that moment that these visions of despair and grief would always be a part of me.

Janice, who still had a firm grip on my left hand, was squeezing it so hard that my fingers were numb, but I had not the heart to tell her. She was so young, and the memories that were being made at this moment were so overwhelming I just wanted to be a help to her, anyway I could. I desired her to feel secure in the midst of the awfulness and if my hand offered her that, so be it.

Everywhere we moved on the deck, tears and prayers were being lifted up to the Lord, and it made me think of Psalm 56 verse 8 which talks about the Lord putting our tears in a bottle. It also brought to mind our church service of yesterday morning. Was it only 12 hours or so ago that we had the awesome ceremony? It now seemed like eons, but the beauty and the simplicity of it brought me peace just then. God had showed up in His people's praise, and He was still in the midst of us even in this calamity; most assuredly a very present help in trouble. 'Thank Ye Lord!'

We were nearing the back of the Boat Deck, and I wondered what our next move would be when suddenly Amos halted and turned to look at us. We girls merged together to be near him. "Ye must stay here near Boat 16 for that is the one ye will be loaded upon."

The four of us turned, and peered at the boat in question, and noticed that it was already being filled. I experienced a brief moment of relief until I realized that they were still just loading woman and children. Quickly, I sought Amos's eyes and in one look knew that he would not be joining us on the boat. He smiled and shook his head to my unasked question. "I cannot be going with ye lass, but I don't want ye ta worry none. I'll be fine."

Janice began to cry now with the realization that Amos would be one of those left behind. Meghan and Eliza Mae also struggled with tears, as did I, and the four of us moved closer to Amos in unison for one final hug. He smiled and gave each of the girls a squeeze on the shoulder which only made our tears really flow. We now understood a bit more the anguish felt by the separated families. There was an ache in the heart that seemed to spread to all parts of the body until your head felt ready to pop off the neck. It was a horrible sad ache and I desperately wanted it to go away because it reminded me too much of the day me Da had left. Without even thinking about it I was beseeching God to bless him wherever he was. Wow, what a difference a day could make in a person's life, and it was all because of Amos.

"Come ladies let us get you aboard." directed Mr. James the Master-at Arms as he navigated young Janice toward Boat 16. She turned quickly before allowing an Able Seaman to put her into the lifeboat and gave Amos a big hug crying, "Thank ye so much!"

Meghan and Eliza Mae did the same and then it was only Amos and I standing there. I could not bear to look at him, so I spoke to an area on his chest.

"Amos, I do not want it ta end like this. There has got ta be a way for ye ta be getting off this ship! I cannot comprehend the fact that I will never be seeing ye again. Oh God, I cannot!" Taking hold of my chin and lifting it up until our eyes met, Amos peered deep into mine, and the genuine tenderness and love conveyed within them caused my heart to miss a beat. "It is gonna be all right lass, believe me."

Gripping his hands in my own I sobbed, "How can ye say it's gonna be all right when so many may perish in this tragedy?"

His blue eyes twinkled as he grinned at me and I was overwhelmed with so many feelings all at once that I did not know what to do or say, but he continued, "Do ye remember, earlier this evening, when I told ya that not one sparrow falls without the Father knowing about it, and does He not love us more than sparrows? I should say He does, and I'll trust whatever His reasons are for allowing such a thing to occur. His ways are higher than ours and because I know Him ta be good, kind, merciful and loving, I also know that He will bring about His purposes, no matter what or how I perceive this misfortune."

Looking down at the deck and scuffing at it with the toe of my shoe and then glancing back at him, I whined, "But it's not fair."

"Life is not fair Shanna Kathryn, and no one ever said it was. In fact, living life takes hard work, but we have a God who is always looking for ways ta make it and us better. Daily, through everything we walk through, He desires to renew our minds and glory by wonderful glory change us into His image. Everything He allows is for relational reasons. He is always looking for ways to draw us close."

Scoffing at his reply, I let go of his hands, "Well this catastrophe surely is not going to endear people ta Him, in fact, I believe more will be set against His existence than anything else. They will say, 'How could a loving God, allow such an awful thing to occur? Therefore God must not exist."

"Shanna Kathryn, there have been travesties of this nature all throughout history, but loss of life does not make God desist. Remember, we are given free will ta do what we desire. Every moment of every day we have choices ta make and for some of those choices we seek the direction of God, but mostly we simply do what we feel will make us happy. Will it surprise ye, ta know that the Titanic received six iceberg warnings yesterday, but they were ignored, and the vessel was given more steam, ta increase her speed? God sent six warnings and they ignored them, but He will receive the blame and be called an unloving God. Humanity is a fickle creature; ever wanting their own way and desiring God ta bless it, no matter what!"

The boat deck was getting crowded and looking about I could read despair in so many faces. Turning back to Amos I implored, "Can't God stop this from happening? Like the Red Sea crossing, can He not stop so many from perishing?"

"Ye forget that many did perish at the Red Sea crossing, for all of Pharaohs' horses, chariots, and horsemen followed the Israelites inta the Sea, as well as his army, and not one of them remained. For some, the Red Sea crossing was a miracle, but for others it was a disaster. It was Pharaoh's hardened heart, and his choice that sent his army after them. The Israelites heeded the Word of God; Pharaoh did not. The Titanic received the

48

warnings and made the decision ta ignore them and now we all suffer the consequence and, for many the cost will be their very lives."

It all made awful sense but still, God is God, is he not? 'Lord why do ya not stop this from happening?' my mind screamed. It was at that moment that I realized the ship was tilting forward. It had been a subtle occurrence at first, but now I really sensed the forward pull and knew things were getting critical.

"Amos, doesn't God love us?"

Reaching for me, he pulled me close for a moment before answering. "Most assuredly He does. Believe me, Shanna Kathryn, when I say ta ye that there are many on record throughout history that have had personal encounters with God in which their lives were dramatically changed in a twinkling. Some went through a horrible ordeal before they believed He was a real and very active part of their lives. In fact, this very night, there are many people being transformed by what is transpiring. The stories of what God is doing ta turn evil inta good are endless. The cowardly are realizing that they are indeed strong. The fearful are finding courage ta help another. The selfish are laying down their lives in a very selfless way even as the prideful are being humbled, though sadly some will never recover from the shame they feel over the choices they made, or the peril they caused. But does God love them any less? Absolutely not! His love is unfailing and endures forever and since I believe that and know this ta be true, I can trust that God's perfect will, will be done, even now."

Pulling out of his embrace, I frowned, "Amos, I don't understand how ye know all these details, like about the warnings and such? Where did ye receive such information? I cannot believe that the crew would have revealed this ta ye with ye being just a passenger and all. How is it that yer so informed?"

Smiling, Amos shook his head saying, "It matters not how I know, Shanna Kathryn, I just do."

"Mum, I need to be getting you aboard the boat." interrupted Mr. James.

Turning, I looked at the man kindly and asked, "May I just have another minute with me friend here?"

He looked at me strangely, and then firmly said, "Don't be long or you will miss your chance to board." Nodding my head, I smiled at him before turning back to Amos.

"We met at Callahan Pond when ye were 13 years old."

"What?"

"Ye need ta get goin', so I thought I would tell ye where we met so ye could leave."

Dumbfounded I frowned, "Amos, we never met at Callahan Pond because the one and only time I was there, was in the winter when I went ice skating with a few friends. It turned inta a dreadful day because I went through the ice. No, if ye would have been there, I would have remembered."

"So one of yer friends pulled ye from the water?"

"Not right away. Everyone was skating and no one saw me go through the ice. They did not realize that I was in the frigid water trying ta find me way out. I thought for sure I was going ta drown then somebody saw me and grabbed me by the hair, pulling me ta safety."

This time Mr. James took me by the arm leading me to the lifeboat, "Sorry mum, but I must insist that you get aboard now."

Tearing free of him I ran and flung my arms around Amos, holding him tight and kissing him on the cheek. I did not want to leave him and I felt all warm inside when I felt his arms engulf me in a hug that nearly squeezed the air from my lungs.

"I don't want ta leave ye Amos, don't make me leave ye!"

He still held me in his arms and I felt him kiss the area by my temple then he put me away from him saying, "Ye have ta go lass. Think of Janice and the others. They need ye Shanna Kathryn."

A hundred different emotions battled within me at that moment. I wanted to go, but I did not want to leave him. I desired to stay, but I also desired to live. I was in turmoil, and he must have sensed that because he quickly picked me up and placed me into the lifeboat before I could say a word. As soon as I was seated next to Janice, Mr. James and two Able Seamen jumped aboard, as others began lowering the lifeboat.

From the Boat Deck, Amos watched us as we were lowered to the ocean below, but before we got too far away he yelled, "Which one or yer friends pulled ye from the pond, Shanna Kathryn?" Tears made wet paths down my cheeks and I shook my head not believing that he was still on the pond subject.

Peering up at him, trying to etch his face into my memory, I cried for all that would be lost this night. Through the mistiness of my tears, the vision of him distorted as if I was underwater looking up and my breath escaped me in a rush and I gasped. I was thirteen years old again and desperately searching for an opening in the ice when I felt my hair being tugged. Looking up through the ice and water, I saw Amos pulling me toward a hole and then I felt his strong hands grabbing me under the arms hauling me out of the frigid water. I lay sputtering and rolling on the ice trying to catch my breath. By the time I had done so, my friends were all around me comforting me and helping me back home. I was freezing and all I could think about was getting warm. Later that night, I remember rousing from a dream of a blue-eyed handsome stranger pulling me from the water. It was only a dream, and I had always assumed that one of my friends had pulled me to safety, although for some reason, the subject was never discussed.

Was it really Amos who had done the deed? But how could that be, he looked the exact same as he does now? Even the clothes were the same and that was over seven years ago. 'Lord, what is going on?' I wondered.

In a soft voice the answer came to my mind as Psalm 91 verse 11 was whispered, "For he shall give his angels charge over thee, to keep thee in all thy ways." And just as quickly, Hebrews chapter 13 verse 2 was spoken, "Be not forgetful to entertain strangers: for thereby some have entertained angels unawares."

Emphatically, my mind rebelled against this idea. There was no plausible way that this could be true. Amos...An angel...Doubt and unbelief tripped one upon the other as question after question raced through my mind along with the events of yesterday. Then I grasped hold of one statement he had made that stood out now, above all the rest. "I know so much about the Word of God because . . . I know the Word of God."

Amos had not been alluding to memorizing the Bible as I had surmised, but to knowing and being on familiar terms with Jesus, because Jesus is the Word of God.

In the book of John, the 14th verse of chapter one states, "And the Word was made flesh, and dwelt among us, and we beheld his glory, the glory as of the only begotten of the Father, full of grace and truth."

As a Christian, I believed that Jesus is the One and Only Begotten Son of God who was born of a Virgin, suffered under Pontius Pilate, was crucified, bearing the sins of man with Him on the cross, before He died and was buried. I firmly believed that on the third day, He rose again and lived among them eating, teaching, and performing more miracles before eventually ascending into heaven where He is seated at the right hand of God, making intersession for us, and waiting for the day of His glorious return.

This is the Word of God he knows! Amazed, I looked up at him and saw him nodding his head and smiling as if he knew the revelation I was having regarding who or what he was. Wonderment coursed through every part of my body, and I felt, for a moment, very much alive and filled with excited awe. Amos is an angel, and that is how he knew me and my friends and the information regarding the Titanic!

A bright smile lit my face, and I began to laugh nervously and wave to him. Still smiling, he waved in return and then disappeared from sight the moment the boat touched the ocean's surface.

My show of exhilaration was short lived as I was quickly brought back to the moment and the dire circumstances surrounding us. I noticed a few of the women looking at me reproachfully. Embarrassed I bowed my head, because these people did not understand my joy. I must have appeared indifferent to the horror transpiring before our very eyes. Even Eliza Mae and Meghan had appeared confused by my display, and though I wanted to shout aloud what I had found out, I understood that I would have to wait for a more opportune time and place to explain myself.

Turning my face away from those in the boat, I closed my eyes and let everything within me praise the Lord for His goodness. I was overwhelmed with thanksgiving and delight, and my spirit just seemed to soar within. It took all that I had to not give voice to my elation!

The persistent clasping of my hand by Janice brought me back to the present and, reassuringly, I rubbed her arm and kissed her forehead as we sat in the shadow of the failing ship hoping to transfer to her some of the peace I was feeling at that moment. I smiled when I felt her grip relax some and was grateful when the Master at Arms ordered the sailors to begin moving our craft away from the ship.

Chapter 12

As our lifeboat began making its way from the Titanic's side, we were able to see clearly just how very bad things really were. It was a haunting sight, to say the least, for the entire bow of the ship was underwater up to the Promenade Deck. The upper decks now teemed with people, and you could hear the anguished shouts and cries of many as one after another realized the predicament of so few lifeboats. I was very humbled again at God's great mercy to see the four of us safely off the ship.

Gunfire, aboard the Titanic which came from the crew trying to control the crowd, caused us both to jump in unison. Upset, everyone in Boat 16 looked at each other anxious and thinking of those that were left behind. It was a bit disconcerting to see the Master-at-Arms jolt at the sound and I observed him looking intently at the other crew members before nodding to them some unspoken arrangement. Things were rapidly going from bad to worse on the Titanic, and the two Able Seamen hastened to put their arms to their oars, maneuvering us further away from the sinking vessel. They knew, we found out later, that when things turned catastrophic with so many people in the water the lifeboats would be easy targets to be swamped by those frenzied souls trying to survive and in their blind desperation; those in the frigid ocean would latch onto anything, even another human being, regardless of the outcome.

Pulling away from the Titanic, we watched in hopeless dismay as her bow and hull seemed to slide lower in the water. It all seemed like a bad dream, one that I kept hoping to awaken from. Hundreds of people swarmed the decks and some were throwing items of furniture into the water before jumping in after the objects thinking they would fare better, I imagine in the frigid sea than on the failing vessel.

A distress rocket pierced the dark night, a final dazzling shimmering plea for assistance from the suffering haughty Queen of the Ocean, but her fate was already sealed. The Word says in Proverbs chapter 16 verse 18 that, "Pride goeth before destruction, and a haughty spirit before a fall." Prideful and haughty were apt adjectives for the Titanic.

In the midst of all the madness, you could hear the strains of music from a band playing somewhere on deck as if this was nothing out of the ordinary, and everything was going to be all right. It was such a compassionate show of charity that the memory of it still gives me goose bumps to this day. Amos had been right in his prediction; people were showing acts of selflessness in the midst of tragedy.

As we continued our course in putting a gap between us and Titanic, Janice leaned near and whispered, "I'm so worried about Amos and all those who will not be able ta board a lifeboat. How will they survive? It is so very cold and the water must be freezing. Why, those jumping in, cannot last long, can they?"

I looked out across the water to where the ghastly scene was still unfolding. We had distanced ourselves from the calamity and it almost seemed now as if we were on the outside looking in. Since we were safe in our little lifeboat, it appeared for the moment that by our ability to escape we were now somehow separated from the wretched situation. You know, like when you hear about a disaster in some other part of the world, and you feel sad for them and what they are going through. But in the same instance, you're glad that it is them and not you. It was a detestable thought, I know, but I am only being honest. Even with many crying softly around me in sadness and despair, I was thanking God that He pulled my friends and me from the pit and set our feet on a rock.

Kissing Janice on the cheek, I whispered, "Don't ye be worrying none about Amos, for that one will be just fine. Let us pray silently for those still on board and in the water. We shall ask God ta have mercy on them and ta send help swiftly." Janice squeezed my hand in agreement and we both quietly prayed.

Only the starry hosts of heaven shined their lights upon us as we floated in the cold Atlantic Ocean, watching the Titanic, who seemed to glow from within, list badly. From where we sat, we were able to, some extent; observe that which was taking place on the decks and right around the ship. We could not make out individual forms floating in the ocean, but all knew many were in the frigid waters. We had seen them jump and now heard their cries for help.

Praying continually for assistance to come, my eyes constantly scanned the scope of the ocean for some sign of aid arriving on the scene, but it was all in vain. It appeared that we were very much alone and adrift in the middle of the Atlantic.

All of a sudden someone gasped, and immediately all eyes were fixed on the ailing vessel. In disbelief and horror we watched as the bow plunged under the water; the surge, knocking many people into the ocean before the weight of the water on the bow caused the forward funnel to collapse. I learned later that many people were crushed when that funnel fell but from where we were that was not discernible with the naked eye.

The cries and screams of those in the water and still on the ship mingled with the sound of iron groaning and ripping apart. The Titanic, it seemed, was making her anguish and woe heard as the once prideful Lady struggled to maintain buoyancy in her rapidly sinking world. She could not withstand the powerful force of the sea, however, and shortly after quarter past the hour of 2:00 a.m. her lights blinked once and then never again. In the space of a couple minutes, the unsinkable Titanic disappeared beneath the ocean's surface plunging to her watery grave.

There were a couple of reports from those closest to the ship when she disappeared from our sight. One allegation was that she never broke up but slid courageously beneath the waves in one piece. The other, from several eye witnesses, claimed she broke in two as the bow was being pulled under, with the stern falling back level to the ocean then filling with water until tilting straight up before steadily sinking out of sight. From where we sat in the darkness, safely away from the suction of the sinking ship and the fear of being pulled under with her, we could hear much of what was taking place. I happen to believe the second claim due, in most part, to the awful sounds of iron ripping before she lapsed into the annals of shipwreck history. Noble Titanic was gone, but her saga of life and death would be remembered for years to come.

The frigid ocean was now filled with hundreds of people struggling to survive, screaming for help, and begging to be saved. (At that time we had no idea how many souls were in the water. It was only later, after the formal inquiries that we found out that more than1500 people lost their lives that fateful night).

One matronly woman aboard Boat 16 asked Mr. James if we were going back to see if we could help save anyone in the water and bring them aboard.

Mr. James was quick to shake his head no. "We cannot go back right now because those in the water will swamp us in our attempts to give them aid. There will be no reasoning with them in their fearful and frenzied state. We will just have to wait and hope that helps comes soon."

I remember closing my eyes desiring to replace the pitiful cries of the lost with fonder memories, but I could not. Letting go of Janice's hand, I covered my ears and began humming a hymn, eager to drown out the wails and moans of the hopeless, but it was a useless attempt, for in the stillness of the night I could hear the splashing and thrashing of those terrified souls as they tried with all their might to hang onto the tenuous grasp of the life they held dear. Their voices rose in anguish and misery at what was happening to them, and their accusations of abandonment toward those of us in the lifeboats caused me to lean over the side and retch. The word, "Murderess!" screamed in my own mind and suddenly I no longer felt separated from the situation but right in the thick of it. By our not going back to save whom we could, we were sentencing those in the water to death. Was that not murder?

I have heard it said, that an ordeal, of any sort, seems to have the ability to change minutes into what seems like hours, and that is what we experienced sitting securely in our lifeboat waiting for help to arrive, while so many others fiercely battled the ocean and the cold, all the while, pleading for the chance to live. "For the love of God, come back and save us!" "I know you can hear me, please save one life!" "How can ya leave us here to die? Come back! Come back!" The chorus of cries came at us from every direction out of the darkness, and we remained unmoving.

Mr. James stood staunchly in his resolution not to return, and we, the passengers in Lifeboat 16, did not argue the matter. Each of us seemed relieved to have the decision taken out of our hands as if the blame could now solely rest upon the Master-at-Arms' competent shoulders.

Janice wept bitterly burying her head into the soft of my neck. While hugging me tightly, she gulped air into her quivering body as her soul-wrenching sobs mingled with the weeping of others in our vessel. I looked to where Meghan was holding Eliza Mae in her arms as that one too, cried out her hearts ache and despair into the waning night. I worried for Eliza Mae as she had seen so much loss in her life already. I wondered if this tragedy would break her. I quickly prayed that it would not.

Chapter 13

As time wore on it seemed that the cries of those in the water appeared to have diminished, in some respect. Perhaps some of the other lifeboats were returning to the scene to help rescue people and once removed, their crying ceased. Hope began to spring anew within me, and I prayed toward that end because in less than an hour the sea grew quiet. I felt strongly that many of those that had been in the frigid ocean had been picked up as it was entirely inconceivable to me to believe that no lifeboats would have returned.

In the dimness of the night, we came upon Lifeboat 6, and it was decided upon to tie up with them and await our fate together. I quickly counted 28 people aboard her and with our 28 that made 56. A sickening feeling of despair grew in the pit of my stomach as I realized that both boats were obviously launched less than full. Such a waste and it was blatantly clear that neither went back to rescue any of the wretched souls floating in the water. "Oh, my God, please let it be that the other boats went back and rescued some, please, let that be the way of it!" my mind screamed silently in distress.

The caverns of the mind are numerous and vast and when one has nothing to do but wait the mind can be an ambiguous place. Sitting in the middle of the ocean in freezing temperatures, not knowing when or if you will be rescued causes your thoughts to wander in and out of the limitless areas of your intellect.

'How long can we float here without food or water if help does not arrive? Would it not have been more merciful to have gone down with the ship than to float out here freezing to death? What if no one has seen our distress rockets or heard our cry for help? What if it takes days for someone to come to our aid? What happens if the weather changes and the winds grow stronger and waves flip our boat? Why did I survive this, and what purpose does my life have that is so different from those that perished? Why did God allow this? Isn't He a God of love? Perhaps those that perished were sinful? He who is without sin cast the first stone. What was it that Amos had said, "We are forever wanting our own way, no matter what, and desiring God to bless it." Why was I saved, not once but twice? How many dead are floating in the dark waters around us? Are there such things as ghosts? Will they try to haunt us because we did not go back to help them? Oh God, send help quickly! What is to become of us? Will I ever see my family again? I miss me Mum! She will be so distraught when she hears of this. Please God comfort my family. Was Amos truly an angel? Yes, he must have been because he seemed to know so much! Why were we singled out for saving? God is not a respecter of persons, yet He sent a messenger to guide us to a lifeboat, why? Thank God that Amos told us to bring our valuables; at least we will not be penniless once we reach shore, if we reach the shore. What will I do once this is over? How can I live the same life I was planning on living, when such a thing as this has occurred, and I have been rescued from it? Life has to have more meaning than just living now. It has to have a specific purpose and plan, no mediocrity for me. I have to have big dreams for a higher purpose of existence. One does not just survive to survive. One survives in order to live...really live...reflectively, intentionally, all the while purposely savoring life to its fullest! Things will never be the same again. Never! Each dawn I see, each breath I take, will be observed and taken with the highest form of thanks-giving in my heart! Oh dear God, I desire to live. Please send us help right away! Please send us help, O Lord!'

We floated in the Atlantic, solemnly and reflectively, for an hour and ten minutes after the Titanic sunk before we caught a glimpse of shimmering light against the starlit sky. It was a signaling rocket from the liner Carpathia. A shout of joy and a collective sigh of relief were heard, and then we waited with newfound hope for her lights to appear on the horizon.

A verse out of the Psalm I had read before I had fallen asleep that night came to me as we waited for our rescue, "God shall help her and that right early."

Tears stung the corners of my eyes as I pondered that verse realizing that it would most likely be dawn by the time the ship reached us.

Chapter 14

Once securely aboard the Cunard Liner Carpathia and heading for New York, we were separated into classes, and it was here that my worries of earlier were confirmed. I quickly estimated the number of steerage passengers to be well under 190, and I felt my heart sink at the lack I saw. There were about as many men rescued as woman, and the number of children I witnessed on deck was under thirty.

What a horrible loss. How will we exist with the knowledge that so many died and we did nothing to give them aid? It was easy to blame Mr. James while seated in the dark, for the reality of the situation was shadowed in the unknown. Now sitting here and blatantly seeing the outcome of our decision in the stark light of the day, one could feel the stalwart hand of guilt and rebuke holding us accountable as well.

We four girls huddled together trying to comfort each other and keep warm. Carpathia's crew came around with blankets and hot beverages which were gratefully accepted. They were busy trying to figure out where they were going to put us for the remainder of the journey.

I watched as Janice scanned the faces of the rescued and knew what she was going to say, "I don't see Amos anywhere on the deck. Do ye think perhaps they have him in another area or do ye think he's...?" Tears burst into her eyes and she was unable to finish saying what, she obviously thought, was apparent.

In the moments before we were brought aboard Carpathia, I had wondered how I would tell the others about Amos being an angel because I desired for them to realize the importance of his showing up like he did and delivering us into the lifeboat. I wanted them to understand that Amos was a reflection of God's love toward us, and I wanted them to know the miracle that got us where we were now.

Taking a sip of my coffee and leaning into the middle of our circle, I spoke softly, "Will ye believe me when I tell ye that Amos is all right and we are not ta worry about him at all?"

"But Shanna Kathryn," frowned Janice, "How can ye say such a thing when it is as plain as the nose on yer face that he is not here with the 3rd class passengers, and I truly doubt they would allow him ta mingle with the first and second class gentry."

Joyful, I continued in a whisper, "Ye are right Janice, he is not here where we can see him, but nonetheless, I believe him near."

Eliza Mae grimaced, "What are ye talking about? Do ye think he's a ghost or something, near but not here?"

"It does sound kind of outlandish, Shanna Kathryn. Can you explain yourself any better?" inquired Meghan.

Nodding my head and taking another sip of coffee, I cleared my throat and came right to the point, "Amos did not perish at sea, and he is not among the rescued because . . . well because . . . he is an angel."

Three pair of incredulous eyes looked at me doubtfully. Eliza Mae was the first to respond. "I believe she is delusional and the wreck has ruined her mind."

"The wreck has not ruined me mind and I am completely sane." I grinned.

"I don't know, Shanna Kathryn, it sounds kind of ludicrous to me too." stated Meghan.

"I believe in angels." Janice said firmly.

Laughing, I reached forward to give her hand a squeeze. "Ye should Janice, because God sent one ta the four of us, and that is how we got off that ship."

Frustrated, Eliza Mae shook her head, "Ye cannot honestly believe what yer saying? There are no such things, as angels!"

"Yes there are and we four beheld one with our own eyes and touched him too."

Meghan's voice of reason broke in, "What makes you think he was an angel, Shanna Kathryn?"

"Not was but is, Meghan, and me reason goes back a few years ago ta when I was thirteen years old..."

Wonder filled Janice's eyes when I finished my tale and she

glowed brightly with awe. "Shanna Kathryn, his being an angel explains how he knew yer name and ours too!"

Meghan, ever level headed, quipped, "Well, I am not saying he is or he isn't until I think this over more."

"That is fine, Meghan, and I want ye ta know that I think it is good that ye desire ta think about it because it really will change how ye think about life and yer part in it knowing that a heavenly being was sent by God ta keep ye in yer ways and bring ye ta safety."

Eliza Mae was still frowning, "I don't understand it? Why would God, send me an angel and not send one ta save me family from the fire or why were we chosen from the many others on the Titanic? How does He pick and chose whom He saves? Explain this ta me, Shanna Kathryn, and then I might be believing in yer angel."

I was taken aback by her response. I had thought we would all be rejoicing together over the goodness of God, and here I was getting all kinds of unbelief. I had not anticipated this when I was deciding on how to tell them. My mind raced down many paths as I sought wisdom from the Word that was within me. Silently, I prayed for counsel and understanding to come upon me so that I could bring forth truth to the situation because I was unsure where to begin. Mentally my thoughts raced through the scriptures in my memory from the book of Genesis forward and then I knew. I would start in the text that is considered to be the oldest in the Bible by scholars. I presented my belief with evidence from the book of Job.

"Eliza Mae, have ye ever read the Book of Job?"

Shaking her head no, she replied "Just bits and pieces here and there, but never start ta finish."

"All right, I just wanted ta make sure ye knew what I was talking about since Job discusses the valid dilemma many have with human suffering. Job was a blameless and upright man fearing God and shunning evil, yet God allowed Satan the power ta touch all he had, but not lay a hand upon his person. So Job's livestock were taken in a raid, and some of his servants were killed, then fire came down from heaven, and his sheep and more servants were killed, and while the messenger of these horrible losses was still speaking, another came ta tell him that a strong wind came from across the wilderness and struck the four corners of the house of his eldest son while he was sharing a meal with his brothers and sisters, and the house fell upon them killing them. And as if that wasn't bad enough, God then allowed Satan ta attack Job's health, because Satan believed that if Job lost everything he held dear, and became so ill that even lying down would be painful, Job would curse God for the pain and evil that had come inta his life. Now, Job was no saint, and he struggled with his feelings and emotions just the same as we do. He even asked, "Why?" on several occasions and received no answer. Then ta top it all off, he was surrounded by some well meaning, but errant friends in the process who believed that blessing was tied ta one's spirituality. Ta them it was obvious, that Job had sinned in an area of his life, and was now reaping the just rewards because God would not punish a good man. Praise be ta God that a bright young lad finally stepped onta the scene, stating that Job's problem was that he had been behaving toward God as though they were equals. He explains that God has been trying ta teach him something through his affliction and that He desired Job ta cry out ta Him for help since there is no one that teaches as He does. This young man goes on ta declare the praises and majesty of God ta Job, setting the stage for God ta intervene in Job's life in a divine but direct way."

Looking deeply into Eliza Mae's eyes, I continued, "Just like He did with us this day. We are unaware of all the circumstances surrounding this tragedy, but God directly intervened for the four of us. Do I understand why so many perished and we were saved? No, and I probably never will, but what I am convincingly sure of is the fact that no matter how many times bad things happen ta good people God is faithful through and through. I also believe He desires for us ta cry out ta Him for help in our affliction. Ta seek Him and ta know Him intimately so that He can lead and guide us throughout our days. We were handed a unique gift when Amos entered our lives. How will we respond? Will we treasure what was a direct encounter with God or will we doubt and accuse and miss this opportunity ta grow and ta live. God loves us and desires us ta be with Him and near Him every step of the way. Will we choose ta attack Him for what we feel is not right or will we choose ta believe that no matter what this life holds, God is more than able ta bring goodness out of it? Ye see, once Job cried out ta God, God answered him and restored ta Job twice as much as he had before, and I believe that Job always carried the memory of those lost ta him in his heart and that with his new family he was a man of much love and affection. I am of the opinion that things were better for the latter children because of the sorrow and pain he had walked through. Who are we ta think that we know what is best for us? We, who cannot see past the moment, continue ta doubt an All-Knowing and All-Seeing God? The God who knows the plans He has for us, plans that are not evil but good, that will give us a future and a hope?"

Eliza Mae looked at me with tears in her eyes. I could see doubt battling with belief as the war within waged upon her face. She was struggling to see her way in this place of decision and my heart longed to reach out and hold her near, but I knew God was in charge of this moment. I waited while she contended with the confliction of her soul.

In turmoil she cried angrily, "God could have intervened for me family and stopped them from dying in the fire, but He didn't. The same goes for what happened here. Your explanation does not help me understand why He saves some but not others. What about their future and their hope for good? If He knows the plans He has for us then what yer telling me is that His plans for me family and all those that were lost here were that they were born only ta one day perish in a horrible way! Is this a good God? I ask ye! Tell me, Shanna Kathryn, if ye think this is merciful, for I do not! I would like it better if there were no God and then I could believe that things were just chance and happenstance, with no rhyme or reason. Believing that there is a

God who controls our destiny and allows some ta suffer and die for no good cause, is a tough piece to chew on."

"Oh Eliza Mae, He is in control, but we still have free will. There were ice berg warnings given ta the Titanic, but her captain failed ta heed them and a disaster resulted. God did not choose this consequence, men did, yet we all have ta live with the misery of that choice. I would be lying if I said I understood why some people live ta a ripe old age and some die young! I do not understand it but I know what happened ta the four of us, and it has made me realize that God is not finished with the work He began. Yesterday, when we were discussing, "Eliza Mae's Tasty Treats", ye yerself made mention of knowing that there is a plan for yer life! Can ye not, in the face of everything that has happened believe that His plan for ye is still unfolding? All things work together for our good Eliza Mae and for the good of all those we will touch one day with our lives. I can trust that He has our best interest at heart even when we walk afflicted. Does God love ye more than yer family that was lost? No. But in His All-Knowing way, He has reached down and saved ye because His plan for ye has the specific need of yer survival in order for it ta play out. Am I in sorrow over what has transpired? Indeed I am, but I can also rejoice in our salvation!"

Eliza Mae hung her head and cried. "I hear what yer saying, Shanna Kathryn, but I am not where yer at just yet."

I reached forward and grabbed her two hands in my own and squeezed them tenderly, before reaching up and placing one of my hands upon her face in a loving, comforting way. "All is well, Eliza Mae. Ye do not have ta believe just because I say so. I trust God ta speak ta yer heart when the time is right."

Sniffling, Eliza Mae nodded her head, and I gave her cheek a tender pat before sitting back to sip my coffee. All at once, I was very tired and every part of me yearned for a place to lie down and rest. I hoped they would find us some place to sleep, and soon.

Chapter 15

For the remainder of our journey, the subject of Amos was, for the most part, not talked about. However young Janice would whisper his name now and then as she praised God for our deliverance.

At 9: 00 p.m. on Thursday, April 18, 1912, the liner Carpathia reached New York, and the details of the disaster began to be heard around the world. For the survivors, there was questioning and inquiries made, as well as the immigration process that needed to take place for many. I sent telegraphs off to my family in Chicago and Ireland so that they would know I survived. Then we waited for the authorities to finish their investigation and questioning so that we could go to our respective destinations and begin to piece together our lives after what we had lived through.

Prior to our questioning, the four of us had privately agreed not to say anything about Amos to those examining the details of what occurred aboard the Titanic and after her sinking. We told the officials all they wanted to know about our experience that night, carefully leaving out any reference to Amos in the process. It was emotionally draining, listening to others describing the events of the tragedy, and every evening we went back to our apartment exhausted and raw from the interrogation of that day. In the quiet of the night, however, I silently marveled at the knowledge that what Amos had shared with me had indeed been what had occurred; the warnings, the speeding up of the ship instead of it slowing down to heed them, the bold courage displayed by many brave souls in the face of death, as well as the tragic loss of so many lives. The inquiries were a humbling process. They did impart to me, though, the importance of being thankful on a regular basis.

It was on our last day of questioning that we had the good fortune of running into Mr. James again. In my quiet time with the Lord, since arriving in New York, it had been impressed upon me to let the Master-at-Arms know that I did not hold him responsible for anything that took place during the tragedy. He had quite a large amount of responsibility to the 28 souls in Lifeboat 16, and I wanted him to know I was thankful for his kind service to us.

The four of us girls were heading out of the building where the inquiry was taking place and the lobby door was held ajar for us by Mr. James. At first he did not recognize us, but when Janice softly told him, "Thank ye, Mr. James." He looked up in surprise and gave each of us a cursory look and then a quick nod.

I was the last one out the door, so I stopped in front of him laying my gloved hand upon his arm and looking him directly in the eye.

"Mr. James, I want ta express me sincere gratitude ta ye for seeing the four of us carefully aboard Lifeboat 16, and also safely away from the dire situation we found ourselves sadly thrown inta. What transpired was regrettable, most unfortunate, and beyond our control, and I desired for ye ta know that ye did a wonderful job keeping us safe from harm. We four are deeply thankful ta ye." I glanced at the others and they nodded in accord.

Turning back to him I watched as he swiped a tear from his eye and sniffed. Attempting a show of manliness, he cleared his throat before returning a hesitant smile. "Thank you mum, for you have no idea how your words have pierced my soul as my mind has been wrought with all kinds of horrible thoughts about myself, and who I am. Only God knows why we lived through what we did, and I take great comfort in your kind words."

"They are from our heart dear sir and delivered with the best intentions for yer bright future."

Clearing his throat again he bit his lip and nodded, "Good day." before turning away and entering the building we had just vacated, the front of which, was a wall of glass. Watching him walk away, I felt grateful that we had the opportunity to see him again and say what we did and then I noticed that he stopped, shook his head and then turned back towards us. Opening the door, he stepped outside and looked around to see if any others were nearby, before approaching us. In a hushed voice he spoke, "This will probably sound absurd to you, but I have not stopped thinking about it since it took place. I am just going to come right out with it and ask, 'Who were all of you talking to and hugging before entering the lifeboat'?"

Janice looked at me fretful as we had collectively decided to leave Amos out of the formal inquiry answers. Eliza Mae frowned and Meghan just shrugged her shoulders. Peering at Mr. James and seeing that there was something more going on, I asked "What do ye mean, Mr. James?"

Tugging at his bottom lip he appeared to struggle for a moment as if debating whether or not to continue on this path of questioning. Finally, he took a deep breath and said; "When you four came to the area around the lifeboat you were all looking up and talking to some area above your heads." he said motioning with his hand to the air above us. "Then this one here," he said pointing at Janice, "turned from me when I was escorting her to the boat and acted like she was hugging someone when no one was there. The same goes for each of you."

Now looking directly at me he went on, "Then you told me that you wanted to say goodbye to your friend, and you stood there talking to no one. At first I thought the trauma of what was taking place had warped your mind somehow, but it appeared you were all experiencing the same delusion. So I asked myself, what did they see and touch that I could not see nor touch?"

Grinning, I looked at Eliza Mae and saw surprise register upon her beautiful face. Janice and Meghan were looking at her too, both in awe of what Mr. James had revealed. Turning to the Master-at-Arms with a joyful smile I asked, "So Mr. James, what is it that ye think we saw and touched?"

Tentatively glancing around, making sure that no one was within hearing distance, he exhaled forcefully and then in resolved determination turned to us whispering, with a mixture of skepticism and hope, "An angel?"

As soon as the words were out of his mouth, Eliza Mae sobbed and fell in a heap upon the ground.

Tears filled my eyes and a lump formed in my throat. I could hardly contain my joy and I struggled to bring forth my question. "Why . . . would ye surmise sir . . . that we were in the company of an angel?"

Momentarily preoccupied by Eliza Mae's reaction, he surveyed the scene as Janice and Meghan bent to comfort our weeping friend. Collecting himself and turning toward me, he held his shoulders back, lifted his head and looked me straight in the eye. "My grandmother, mum, in her youth she had an angelic encounter that altered her life forever. Through the years I have heard many tales of other angelic encounters and since most of them happen in conjunction with disasters, I had wondered how many of the passengers and crew would witness angels, the moment I heard we had hit an iceberg."

My thoughts were alive with praise, 'O' my God, Yer so good to us!'

Beaming brightly, I confirmed the Master-at-Arms suspicions, "Well Mr. James, we were indeed, having an angelic encounter, however, we did not know that he was not seen by any others than ourselves, until this very moment. In fact, I did not realize he was an angel until after we were aboard the Lifeboat and being lowered onta the ocean."

Eliza Mae's sobs turned to dry hiccups and delight radiated upon her face. I knew that she had come to some kind of revelation regarding Amos, God, and herself.

Relief flooded Mr. James's countenance, and I watched as he closed his eyes and took a deep relaxing breath. Opening them, he stared intently at me. "Your angel brought you to the Lifeboat I was manning, so I take that as a direct assignment from God. He insured your safety to me, in a roundabout way, and I find that most satisfying."

I brushed the tears away that were streaming down my cheeks because of the greatness of what God was doing in all our lives just then. I felt so loved by Him at that moment that I wanted to sing out with all the joy I was experiencing. Just as the Israelites had broken into a song of praise as they watched the Red Sea swallow up their enemy, my soul was magnifying the Lord from within for the goodness He had shown toward us. He loves us! He truly loves us!

With much enthusiasm, I squeezed the hand of Mr. James, "Sir, yer loved without a shadow of doubt by the Creator of all things! Run with this knowledge and live a life that is full and pleasing unta Him! Ye were born for greatness, Mr. James! Remember that, from this day forward, and do not waste the opportunity ye have been given. We have all received a second chance; let us live in such a way that reflects it!"

"Amen to that mum! Amen."

Mr. James turned to Eliza Mae and helped her to stand. Smiling at her, he whispered something, then squeezing her hand; he nodded to each of us before heading back into the building.

Eliza Mae stood there crying again, but a content smile was on her lips.

"What did he say ta ye, Eliza Mae?" inquired Janice.

Gulping to take a shaky breath, Eliza Mae wiped at the tears in the corner of her eyes before answering, "He said, 'Blessed are those who have not seen and yet have believed.' He obviously knew my doubt and was telling me that even though he had not seen Amos, based on our eyewitness accounts, he could believe what we saw and touched with our own hands. He was telling me not ta be a Doubting Thomas."

Meghan wiped at the tears in her eyes, sniffed and changed the subject, "Well, I do not know about the rest of you, but I am one hungry young lady and I make the suggestion that we try to get some supper soon. What do you say?"

Consenting to her advice, we gathered ourselves together and walked away from the building of our questioning and the investigation. For four, Irish women, who had boarded the Titanic a few weeks ago, life would never be the same. The revelation that had taken place moments before was awesome and exciting. God was true and as real as our next breath. He loved us and saved us from one of the worst oceanic disasters and, knowing that He was not finished with us, gave me goose bumps. We strolled in silence all the way to the little diner we had stumbled upon our first night here. The establishment was spotless, the food was delicious, and the matron who ran the diner was kind and courteous.

Chapter 16

The dawn of morning would see me beginning my journey to Chicago, and Janice being collected by her family. Eliza Mae and Meghan were in the process of locating a permanent place to reside, while both continued looking for work. White Star Line had put us up temporarily into a furnished apartment, but that arrangement was soon coming to an end.

Meghan had a scheduled interview with a school in two days, and Eliza Mae had applied at a couple of bakery shops in order to acquire the skills that would one day allow her to branch out on her own. The two of them had decided they would remain in each other's company until such a time as one or the other found work, and then, depending on the location, they could determine if their paths were to continue on together or if they would strike out on their own.

Over dinner, we discussed the ongoing inquiry and the questioning of that day, our plans for the future, and our desire to remain in contact with one another after going our respective ways. But like a curious kitten, who keeps returning to the ball of yarn in a basket, seeking to pull it out, and bat it around the floor willy-nilly, our thoughts wandered across what we were actually discussing, and it teased the desire to delve deeper into what was really on all our hearts; the newfound affirmation of what had transpired aboard the Titanic.

It was only after dessert had been consumed and we were sipping our coffee did the topic, so close to all our hearts come to light.

"I am in awe, of the knowledge that God sent Amos ta guide us off that ship." Eliza Mae murmured before continuing, "I have been so angry with Him, since the loss of me family. I had quit going ta church for I wanted nothing ta do with Him nor His religion. I spoke at Him regularly complaining, and telling Him how awful He has been ta me and how He was an unloving God ta allow such a thing ta happen ta innocent people. I even told meself that He did not exist, yet I always knew in me heart that He did. I was just too hurt and bitter and it was easier that way. I do not understand the why of it but for some reason the why of it no longer matters. I now desire ta know what He has saved me for."

Reaching forward, I grabbed her hand and squeezed it, "For relationship, Eliza Mae; simple relationship. He loves ye and desires ta commune with ye and ta be one with ye. That is what it has been about since the beginning of time, and we, with our human concepts and limited knowledge, seem ta distort it more often than not. We take a good thing and twist it out of shape until it resembles something we can understand, or think we understand, all the while believing the distortion over the simple truth. Love. . . It's all about love."

It was at that moment, sitting in that diner with my friends, that I knew; I would never marry, nor have children, but that I would spend my life seeking Him and sharing what I found with others. It would be a life full of intimacy, relationships, adventures, challenges, difficulties, inspiration, love and contentment. It would be a lifetime of nurturing and growth and there would be seasons of trials and the opportunities to persevere through them. There would be times of loneliness and great happiness, times of sorrow and great joy, hard work and comfort, but peace through it all.

As I sat back and looked around the table at the others as they chatted gaily together, I praised God for what had happened on the Titanic. I was not praising Him for the disaster and the loss of life but for the revelation about me Da, for the friends I had made, for Amos, and for coming out of the tragedy with a purpose and a plan.

Prior to the events of April 14th and 15th, 1912, my goal was to find another job, most likely meet a man and marry, have a handful of children and raise them in a suburb of Chicago. Not that that would be a bad thing, it was just that I had given no real focused thought to my future before. Now, however, I knew what my purpose was and how I would live my life; by design and intentionally for Him.

I felt like young David must have felt when Samuel prophesied over him that one day he would be King over Israel. You have this feeling like, I know what I will be doing, but how do I get from being a shepherd boy tending sheep to a Warrior King leading mighty men? It can overwhelm you and fetter the mind but that is exactly where the intimacy plays its part. By drawing close to the One who made the plans in the first place, you will learn how to go from where you are now to where you need to be. Content with that thought, I smiled reaching for my coffee.

Finishing off the last of it, I listened as Janice began sharing excitedly that she was looking forward to seeing her cousin Carole Jean on the morrow. She was extremely giddy in the telling of how the last time they had been together her cousin, had just gotten married and was moving to America. They had hugged and Carole Jean had whispered that as soon as she could she would send for her to join them once they were settled and in a home of their own. It had been two years since the two had seen each other, and she could hardly wait as the girls were more like sisters than cousins, and the time apart had seemed so long. She got misty eyed talking about how she could have missed the opportunity altogether if Amos had not come along when he did.

It got quiet for a moment and then Meghan glanced out the window of the diner and gasped in surprise. "I think I just saw Amos!" she exclaimed pushing herself away from the table and heading toward the door. I quickly counted out some cash for our supper and left it on the table before following the others out into the night.

Chapter 17

The evening air was brisk and gas lights were afire sending their glowing luminosity up and down the street. Many shopkeepers still had their stores opened, hoping to catch a few patrons on their way home from work. Their interior lights illuminated the sidewalk as well.

Meghan raced this way and that down the street and sidewalk maneuvering in and around others that were intent upon their own coming and going.

Hastily following her lead, we desired to know if she really did, in fact, catch a glimpse of Amos. Neither of us saw what she thought she saw, but we pursued based upon her startled declaration.

All of a sudden she went around the corner of a building and moved out of sight. For a moment, I was unsettled by her disappearance, but then I shook it off knowing that if it was in fact Amos she was pursuing, no harm would come to her.

The three of us burst around the corner after her only to be brought up short by Meghan herself. She was standing in the middle of an alleyway looking about her as if confused and out of sorts. Turning to us she looked dazed. "I know I saw him and I know that he went in this direction, but it is as if he disappeared right before my eyes. It was Amos I was following, I tell you! It was him!"

Janice spoke up, "We believe ye Meghan. If ye say ye saw him, then ye saw him and that is that."

Peering around the alley, I realized that the only reason Amos would have directed us to this area would be for a God reason. "Ladies, since we know who and what Amos is, it makes good sense ta believe that we have been divinely directed here, so let us have ears ta hear and eyes ta see, all right?"

Determined, the four of us travelled down the darkened alleyway carefully looking and listening for whatever it was that God

wanted us to find. The farther away we walked from the main
street with its lights and people the more anxious I became.

Silently, I prayed that whatever it was we were supposed to find
would show itself because I was ready to turn around and head
back. It was grim and scary here, and I imagined, more than a
few times, that little beady eyes were staring at us from the
shadows and monitoring our every move. I nearly jumped out
of my skin when Eliza Mae screeched in fright in the darkness.
There was a scrambling noise then she cried out triumphantly, "I
found it!"

Running toward her and the sounds of her scuffling, we were
surprised to find her struggling with a rowdy youngster. Speaking
consolingly to the resisting waif, Eliza Mae tried soothing the
child, all the while intentionally leading the frantic soul back
out of the dark alleyway and into the light.

In the illumination of the gas lamps, we viewed the sought out
one and were astonished to see the cutest little boy staring back
at us with the biggest hazel eyes. He was shaking from head to
toe and fear was etched upon his little round dirt smudged face.
I guessed his age to be around six or seven.

While the rest of us looked on, Eliza Mae began mothering
him, taking the hem of her dress and wiping at the dirty cheeks
and smoothing his brown tussled hair into place, all the while
cooing at him, trying to calm him down. "What is yer name love
and where are yer parents?" she inquired when she had finished
her ministrations.

Shaking his head back and forth, he began to cry.

Eliza Mae gathered him into an embrace, and he wrapped his
little arms about her shoulders, squeezing them and burying his
small face into the nape of her neck.

"There, there, child, it's going ta be all right. Hush me little
one. It'll be okay. Hush now and tell Eliza Mae yer name."

Crying and shaking nonstop in her arms, he muttered, "Ed. . .
Eddy".

Stroking his brown hair, she rocked and cooed to him soothing
him with her tender voice and gentle embrace. The three of us

looked on, not exactly sure how to be of service to the two of them, but desiring to help, I whispered, "Let's pray." and at the nod of the others, we clasped hands and bowed our heads.

"Dear Lord, we praise Ye for leading us ta little Eddy, and we thank Ye for letting us find him. We know that it is what Ye desired and now we ask for direction as ta what ta do next. Lead and guide us in the proper course ta take O' Lord. And Lord, please calm his little spirit within him so that we can best help him, in the name of Jesus we pray. Amen."

"Amen." the others echoed.

Eliza Mae smiled her gratitude to us as she pulled out of the embrace and standing little Eddy in front of her so that she could better view him, she inquired, "Have ye eaten, love?"

With a quick shake of his head that he had not, she turned to look at us with a decision in mind and replied, "Then that is the first order of events. We will put some delicious food in yer belly, all right?"

Smiling, he nodded, and taking her hand the two of them turned and headed down the street in the direction of the diner we had just vacated.

Sitting with a nourishing plate full of roast beef, potatoes, and green beans, we laughed as Eddy took a hearty swig of cold milk leaving behind, as evidence, a perfect milk moustache on his upper lip. His satisfied sigh and grin melted all our hearts and each of us swiped at our tears that threatened to fall.

As Eddy munched away at his supper, Eliza Mae plied him with questions, "How long have ye been hiding in the alleyway?"

Chewing and then swallowing, he shrugged, "Not sure, 'bout a week?"

"How old are ye, Eddy?"

Between bites of food he managed, "Seven mum, almost eight."

"Where have ye been sleeping at night?"

Munching on a mouthful of roast beef, he paused, "I don't sleep at night. I sleep during the day right where ya found me. At night, I stay awake, look for food, and try to keep out of sight as there are persons that roam about that aim to be cruel to me."

Listening to little Eddy share, I remembered the feeling of being watched as we walked down that alley and I could just imagine the sort of characters that roamed there at night. I shuddered at the thought and silently gave praise to God that Eddy had been found.

"Where are yer parents Eddy?"

When Eliza Mae asked about his parents, little Eddy put his fork down, placed his hands in his lap and shrugged his shoulders.

"When was the last time ye saw 'em?" Janice inquired.

Downcast, he just shrugged again.

Meghan had been listening and watching Eddy's responses and the sensible wisdom of a teacher came out as she asked, "Eddy, were you on the Titanic? Is that why you don't know where your parents are?"

Hazel eyes filled with fear and tears as he nodded his head.

The four of us exchanged knowing glances as we realized that this child had probably been separated from his family on the Titanic and placed aboard a lifeboat without anyone to care for him. Once aboard Carpathia, they would have united if they had survived. If not, upon leaving the liner, he could have easily escaped the notice of the port authorities in all the commotion. I knew what was required. We needed to get in touch with the authorities to have them try and find out if there was any family on either side of the ocean.

Eliza Mae looked at me as we had come upon the same conclusion, and, at her nod, I left the table to talk with the matron of the establishment. I explained what we thought had taken place and asked her to send someone for the authorities. Moved to compassion she sent her son on the mission and then handed me some fresh baked oatmeal cookies, "For the child." she said.

Thanking her I walked back to the table noticing that Eliza Mae had coaxed him into finishing his meal and when I placed the three oatmeal cookies in front of him his eyes widened in obvious delight at the unexpected treat, causing us all to laugh.

Eddy had just finished dunking the last bit of cookie into his glass of milk when two uniformed policemen arrived at the diner with the matron's son. Seeing us sitting in the corner, they wandered over taking off their dress caps as they approached our table.

Eliza Mae rose to stand next to Eddy placing a protective hand upon his shoulder as she addressed them. "Officers, thank ye for coming so quickly. This here is Eddy, and we believe that he is a survivor of the Titanic, like the four of us, but has been separated from his family. We found him this evening down an alleyway and brought him here for sustenance. We knew that someone must be looking for him and we sent for ye straightaway."

I watched as the younger of the two policemen could not keep his eyes off of Eliza Mae as she spoke. He was a tall, brawny, good-looking man with red hair and a splatter of freckles across his face. Cornflower blue eyes intently surveyed the situation and all of us in a moment, but he seemed to land with pleasure back on Eliza Mae.

I smiled realizing that the man had a keen interest in our blonde haired friend, and I wondered what God was up to. So lost in my own musings, I nearly missed what the older man was saying to Eliza Mae.

"We are so swamped down at the station with this Titanic disaster that we have not even had the chance to begin looking for him. He was listed among the surviving passengers inventory from Carpathia, but since their arrival he has been unaccounted for. No one from his family survived, but he does have relatives in England that have been summoned and should be arriving here in the next week or so. In the meantime, I do not know what to do with him. Our orphanages are full and since this is a temporary thing it would be nice to keep him out of them."

Eliza Mae volunteered. "He can stay with me sir until his people arrive. I am planning on finding work and settling here, so it would be of no inconvenience ta me ta care of him, for the time being."

The older man heaved a sigh of relief at having this dilemma taken out of his hands. Turning to the younger man, he said,

"Officer O'Reilly will escort you ladies back to your lodgings and gather all the proper information from you. He will check up on you everyday to make sure that your needs are met. You are doing us a great service and we will help pay for anything you have need of. I am sure the young laddie could be using some new clothes and such, so Officer O'Reilly will be coming around in the morning to see to those needs, if this is satisfactory to you miss?"

Eliza Mae blushed and nodded her head. It seemed as though she had only just noticed the young handsome officer and one could see the surprise and delight register upon her beautiful face.

Meghan, Janice, and I exchanged a knowing look and we grinned from ear to ear as Officer O'Reilly took up one hand of Eddy's while Eliza Mae grabbed the other and proceeded to lead the way out of the diner.

God so amazed me how He could take a disaster, such as the one we had lived through and bring new life from it. For in Officer O'Reilly, I saw a chance at something wonderful and new for Eliza Mae. It made me think of the scripture in John where Jesus says, "Verily, verily, I say unto you, except a corn of wheat fall into the ground and die, it abideth alone: but if it die, it bringeth forth much fruit."

While living life we have the tendency to hold onto bits and pieces of emotional matter that really has no value or benefit to us or others. There just seems to be this obligation and need to keep it close at hand. Imagine holding onto three kernels of corn and keeping them within your fist night and day, never putting them down. You open your hand and there they lie, unchanged day after day, month after month, year after year. They simply remain three little kernels of corn. You know the benefits which can come from releasing them into the dirt, but you are afraid that in doing that, something might happen to them, so you just keep them safe and near and continue to hope that they will grow where they are. Yet the reality is that in order for there to be any kind of change, the seed must be planted into the ground. If only we could understand how close we are sometimes in our lives to the wonderment of a refreshing new reality by being willing to simply let go of what we are hanging onto, good or bad, and trusting it into God's capable hands.

Eliza Mae had done that and perhaps she already tastes the fruit of her surrender. Like me, she had laid down her bitterness and anger burying them deep in the soil of forgiveness and could now look forward to a healthy harvest.

It had felt good and right to me to be angry at me Da, yet in the seeming rightness of it, it was just emotional matter that did not benefit me at all. Only after I covered my bitterness with forgiveness, did I reap the benefit that was meant for me. It would be interesting to watch and see what transpires between the officer and Eliza Mae.

Chapter 18

Little Eddy was sleeping soundly in Eliza Mae's bed after a refreshing bath. She had opted to sleep on the sofa for the night to give him the chance to get a good night's sleep. The four of us marveled at what had come about that evening with the sighting of Amos, which had led us to finding Eddy. There was not a doubt in any of us, that it was he that had guided us down that alley.

Quietly, we conversed amongst ourselves, that finding the child was just as important to us as it had been to Eddy. God, it seemed, was teaching us to listen and obey; in fact as we discussed the matter in depth, it appeared that our entire journey had been about that. We had needed to listen and obey Amos at every step and turn, for in doing so, we became survivors of one of the worst oceanliner tragedies of our time. If we had stopped and deviated at all from what Amos had commanded of us, we, in all likelihood, would not be here now. There was so much to be thankful for.

Talking late into the night, not wanting the evening to end since Janice and myself would be departing on the morrow, we laughed and cried over all that we had been through together. Then promising each other that we would keep in touch and write regularly, we went off to bed where sleep visited us after a time.

Our day dawned with Officer O'Reilly bringing us fresh baked donuts from his brother and sister-in-law's bakery. A coincidence; we didn't think so and much to the young officer's chagrin, we all busted out into laughter with Eliza Mae finally giving in and saying to him, "I'll be telling ye all about it one day." At her winsome smile, he shrugged and joined our merriment while munching on one of the tasty donuts.

Later, on the sidewalk, we all cried as we watched the reunion embrace between Carole Jean and Janice. Carole Jean's husband stood by holding a hat in his hands beaming with love at his wife's happiness as the two girls hugged, laughed, kissed, and cried all the while talking over the other in their enthusiasm to be together. I was thrilled for Janice, she seemed so happy. I prayed that her life would not be terribly affected by the Titanic disaster. Her faith was deep and I felt sure that she would always remember the grace that was shown to us thus enabling her to rise above the horror that she experienced.

Introductions were made and more hugs exchanged before Carole Jean's husband reminded us and the two cousins that they were on a strict time schedule. Holding Janice in a loving embrace I kissed her cheek and cried when she squeezed me tight. "Oh Shanna Kathryn, I'm gonna miss ye so much!" she wailed.

Tears flowed freely from my eyes at her words and I felt my heart in my throat, "I love ye Janice always remember that."

She smiled and placed a kiss on my cheek, before turning away to hug Eliza Mae, Meghan, and Little Eddy. With the goodbyes out of the way, she slid into the back seat of the taxicab followed by Carol Jean and her husband. We all waved as we watched them drive away.

A taxicab was hailed for me as well and after a round of hugs and kisses to Eliza Mae, Meghan, and Little Eddy, I climbed into the vehicle that would take me to the train station. Wiping the road dust off of the seat with my gloved hand, I settled into my place looking forward to my first ride in an automobile while enjoying the sites of New York City.

Chapter 19

On board the train and heading toward Chicago, I closed my eyes and dozed for a time. Upon awakening, I was much surprised, to find that the seat next to me had become occupied while I slept. Wiping at the sleep in my eyes and patting at my hair, I turned toward the one sitting next to me and my heart leapt within me.

"Amos!" I exclaimed.

Those startling blue eyes I remembered so well pierced my heart with their gaze. "Hello, Shanna Kathryn. I asked the Father if I could let ye see me and He said yes."

Heat flooded my being as I laughed and reached for his hand to give it a hearty squeeze. "I was dreaming about ye, just now."

"Ye don't say?"

Nodding my head, I bit my lower lip and continued, "It was as if I was seeing me life like a silent film. Different pictures of different times of me life and strangely enough ye appeared in many of the frames. Even though I was unaware of ye during them, ye were there."

Closing my eyes I tried to bring to mind an example to share with him, and smiling I opened them, meeting his sparkling gaze.

"Like when I was six and learning ta ride a bicycle. Me brother was teaching me, and I was struggling ta keep it moving and upright and then I started heading toward the ditch and certain danger when suddenly the bike was steadied and I was turned away from the ditch and able ta stop without a problem. I turned around ta look at what I had escaped from, and ye were there, but I did not remember that until now."

"And that is as it should be. I am but a ministering spirit sent forth as the Father instructs ta keep ye in all yer ways."

Playing with a button on my dress and no longer looking at him I inquired, "This is the last time that I will see ye here on earth, isn't it?"

"It's the last time ye will see me but not the last time that I'll see ye."

Thinking about that I smiled and looking up at him I whispered, "For some reason, I'm all right with that."

Amos took my hand in his and brought it to his lips for a kiss, which caused my eyes to fill with tears. He was a representation of the love of God toward me, and my heart nearly burst with the overwhelming thought of it. A verse from the Song of Solomon came to mind, 'My beloved is mine and I am His.'

Closing my eyes and savoring that thought, I whispered to Amos, "Thank ye for all ye have done for me and will continue ta do. Words cannot convey the deep- felt appreciation I have."

His fingers caressed my cheek as he whispered in return, "It is truly me pleasure, Shanna Kathryn."

Opening my eyes, I lost myself staring, into his shining blue ones. I wished that somehow I could fix their color into my memory. Then I realized that because Amos was an expression of God to me, I would have no need since He would always be a part of my life. As if perceiving my thoughts, Amos grinned and squeezed my hand before leaning forward to kiss my forehead.

"I'll be seeing ye!"

Smiling and nodding my head, I sat back and feeling drowsy leaned my head upon his shoulder and fell instantly asleep. When I awoke, sometime later, I was alone in my seat, but I knew I was not really alone and a calmness I have never before felt in my life flooded my being and I was content.

Epilogue

Over the years I have awakened, on many occasions to the nightmares of people crying and begging for help. I know that what came to pass aboard the Titanic and immediately after her sinking remains to this day a significant part of my life.

For many years I kept in touch with Janice, Eliza Mae, and Meghan. We were able to get together a few times and we always reminisced about Amos. Janice went on to art school and became a local artist in the area she lived. She met her husband Daniel at an art fair when he, much attracted to a painting of some rolling hills in Ireland, struck up a conversation with her as he paid for the painting. They married six months later and went on to have four beautiful children.

Eliza Mae did, in fact, marry Officer O'Reilly and after working in his brother's bakery for a few years learning the ins and outs of business owning, struck out on her own and opened a confections shop across town. She specialized in making individual cakes, cookies, and candies as well as wedding cake masterpieces. Her talents were sought after by many families of prestige in the New York society. They had three children and lived in an apartment above their business. It was a good match all the way around.

Meghan did indeed get a teaching position. She taught World History in a private school for girls and was a favorite among the students. She brought history alive with her matter of fact knowledge of ancient times and being a survivor of the Titanic only added to her appeal. She married a fellow teacher, named Donald, and they had one daughter.

I never did share with the others about seeing Amos again on the train for when it was all said and done, I was not sure I did not dream the whole thing.

I did dedicate my life to the Lord and have served Him with all my heart for the past sixty plus years. It has been a life of adventure, faith, and love. It has been filled with caring for others; helping those in need, and bringing a message of hope to the downtrodden. It has not been perfect by any means, but I have trusted the One who gave me a second chance so long ago, and I have to say that I would do it all over again.

I take pleasure in traveling and have trekked all over the United States sharing the truth of the gospel with those in need. I almost said no to ocean travel after what had transpired on the Titanic. But my enthusiasm to visit the Holy Land surpassed my fear and I have traveled by sea on many occasions. Never have I again experienced a night like the night of April 14th and the morning of April 15th, 1912 and I give thanks to God for that.

Authors Note

This novella started when my daughter came home in 2003 with a Language Arts assignment to compose a short story about being a survivor of the Titanic. I thought that this was a fascinating idea and decided to try my hand at writing one as well.

My journey began when I picked up a pen and started to jot down some information. I did a rough outline of a story, created my characters by picking out their ages, and making up four names for my heroines. I used only the first names in the telling of my story as last names seemed unimportant to the tale.

Being gifted with an overly active imagination and a penchant for daydreaming, I have many novels in the works but before one is finished, I get another idea and move on to that. Wanting to complete one of them, I prayed in December of 2009, and asked the Lord which storyline He would have me finish and was clearly told, The Titanic account.

Excited to have a direction, I continued on that course. This account was only meant to be a short story, 1500 words or less, but by the grace of God it turned into a 30,000 plus word novella.

What I planned when I started and where I ended up were different, but I like where it ended up. I firmly believe in angels and angelic encounters (having had my own) and from Shanna Kathryn's first waltz with Amos I knew the direction the story would take. I also know that God is into restoring individuals through the truth of His Word, so His redemptive message was a must in my tale.

I hope you enjoyed this Titanic journey as much as I did. The two online sites I used for my research were www.encylopedia-titanic.org and www.titanic.com. Blessings to you.

Kelly Ann Reed
www.kellyannreed.com
www.nightofdestinybook.com

Acknowledgements

I first and foremost want to give thanks to God Almighty for the wonderful gift of forgiveness we have through the life, death, and resurrection of Our Lord Jesus Christ. The freedom that is found through forgiveness is so liberating I felt the need to share it.

I desire to thank my husband Craig for his wonderful artwork (he designed the cover), his love and encouragement throughout my writing process, and for his unending faith in the potential of this story. I love you babe!

Next, I give thanks to my children, Kyle and his wife Melissa Reed, and JoEllen and her husband TJ Couture. You four make my heart so proud and I thank you for all your help, love, and support! I am a blessed mother.

A special thank you, to you few, who read my story while it was a work in process, and desired copies of your own. You blessed me with your sweet words of praise and I thank you all!

Sincere thanks to the Clan Jankowski, my family. You have all waited so long for this moment. All I can say is "Woo up, Woo up!" and "I love you!"

To my Editor; Janis Lord and to my Publisher; Mick McArt, I have a deep appreciation. God truly brought us together, and for that I am thankful.

And I cannot write a story about something as tragic as the Titanic disaster and not acknowledge every life on board that vessel. From the least to the greatest their stories survive into the future, reminding us that we are all connected in a very real way.

CPSIA information can be obtained at www.ICGtesting.com
Printed in the USA
BVOW010916140512

290014BV00004B/6/P